A DOG IN THE MANGER AND OTHER CHRISTMAS STORIES

A DOG IN THE MANGER AND OTHER CHRISTMAS STORIES

Jim Simons

ROWMAN & LITTLEFIELD
Lanham • Boulder • New York • London

Published by Rowman & Littlefield
A wholly owned subsidiary of The Rowman & Littlefield Publishing
Group, Inc.
4501 Forbes Boulevard, Suite 200, Lanham, Maryland 20706
www.rowman.com

16 Carlisle Street, London W1D 3BT, United Kingdom

British Library Cataloguing in Publication Information Available

Library of Congress Cataloging-in-Publication Data

Simons, Jim, 1957–
[Short stories. Selections]
A dog in the manger and other Christmas stories / Jim Simons.
pages cm
ISBN 978-1-4422-4182-4 (cloth : alk. paper) — ISBN 978-1-4422-4183-1 (pbk. : alk.
paper) — ISBN 978-1-4422-4184-8 (electronic)
1. Christmas stories. I. Title.
PS3619.I562866A6 2015
813'.6—dc23
2014030104

Printed in the United States of America

To the people of St. Michael's of the Valley
My flock, my friends, my inspiration.

CONTENTS

Introduction   ix

1 A Dog in the Manger   1

2 Little Brown Bats and Silly Voices   15

3 Angels Unaware   29

4 Little Miss Christmas Tree   43

5 The Three Wise Guys   61

6 Personal Care Pageant   77

7 St. Michael   93

8 Comfort and Joy   105

9 Renovations   117

10 The Gift Giver   131

11 We Three Kings   139

12 I'll Be Home for Christmas   155

About the Author   167

INTRODUCTION

"'Thou shalt not' might reach the head, but it takes 'Once upon a time' to reach the heart."

—Philip Pullman

Everybody loves a good story. Stories are essential to our existence. They are one of the ways we know who we are. Sit around the table at the holiday and the family stories begin to flow about how Dad once tied the Christmas tree to the car roof and tied the doors shut at the same time, or the time Aunt Mabel brought a pie for Christmas that was horrible, but we all ate it so she wouldn't be offended. The stories may not tell of significant events but they tell us about ourselves.

I never knew my maternal grandfather. He was killed in a mine disaster in 1944, when my mother was still a child. But the story of what happened is important to me. I often listened to my mother and my aunt and uncles tell snippets of it and once spent a day in the library reading old newspaper accounts so I would understand what happened. I did this because, even though I didn't know him, his story is a part of my story.

Jesus told a lot of stories. Stories about everyday events like losing a coin, finding a sheep, or going to a wedding banquet. He also told some pretty surprising stories about a Samaritan who was compassionate and a father who threw a party for his ne'er-do-well son. One of the reasons Jesus does this is because stories tend to be easier to remember and are consequently repeated more easily. If a person is asked to recite the Beatitudes most would have some difficulty, but asked to tell the story of the "Prodigal Son" most believers can come up with a pretty accurate rendition. But he also used stories because, as Philip Pullman says, they touch the heart.

Christmas is about a story. It's a story that is as unbelievable as it is true. It's a story about a pregnant virgin, angelic visions, shepherds that walk away from their sheep, and a group of Persian magicians who figure out what's going on long before anyone else.

I was ordained to the priesthood in the Episcopal Church in 1985. As Christmas Eve approached I made a decision that instead of preaching a sermon I would write and tell a story. I have done this almost every year since then and the stories included here represent about half of what I've written.

They are fiction. Like most writers I have borrowed anecdotes from my own life and those of friends. I have conflated experiences and characters that are real, but the stories remain fiction. (There's a joke in the parish that every year at least one person who hears the story is convinced that it's about them.) I want to convey, in this narrative form, the truth about Christmas: that God sent his son into the world; that we are not alone; that there is reason for hope and faith; and, ultimately, that regardless of the circumstances of our lives, God loves us.

It has been pointed out to me that half of the stories included either revolve around or have some reference to a Christmas pageant. I was surprised by this. I think it's because a pageant is a kind of story within a story and allows the characters I've created to enter into it in an incarnational way. It allows them to be the Christmas story.

All of these stories stand on their own, although several are set in the same fictitious town and some characters overlap. I should also say that the narrator in some cases is male and in others female.

This has truly been a labor of love for me and I hope you find a sense of hope and blessing as you read them. I hope they touch your heart.

I

A DOG IN THE MANGER

"I want to put Jesus in the manger!"
"You did it last year. It's my turn."
"No, I'm the oldest. I get to do it."
"Well, I'm the youngest; I think I should!"
Maggie grabbed the figure from Jack and accidentally dropped
it facedown on the hard floor.
"Now you've done it," cried Jack.

This is the story about how I found Jesus, literally.

First, I guess I should tell you about the dog. We had a dog, a big old thing we called "Bear," who mostly lay around the house breathing. Yeah, he would get up occasionally to go out or eat, but at his age, he was basically in hibernation mode most of the time. He went on to his reward last winter, and we missed him a great deal. The next thing I knew, the wife and kids were spending time on the Internet looking for another one. One day, my wife called me at the office.

"I found a dog for us," she said.

"I don't want a dog," I replied.

"Why not?"

"Because they're a lot of work, that's why, and the kids have never had to really take care of one. Bear came to us when he was older. They don't know what's involved."

"But this is such a cute little puppy."

"Puppy?" I exclaimed. "Please don't get a dog, and please don't get a puppy."

Sparky was waiting for me when I got home that evening. She was a three-month-old collie.

"Annie," I whined, "I told you I don't want a dog."

Just then, the kids came bouncing down the stairs. "Daddy, Daddy did you see Sparky?" they screamed, even though the dog was standing on its back paws with its front ones at my waist.

"Can we keep her? Can we? Can we?"

"Annie!" I exclaimed.

"Don't worry, Jack, she's only here on a trial basis."

I knew what that meant. This dog was never leaving.

It wasn't that Sparky was bad; she actually had a rather sweet disposition. It was just that she had so much, well, energy.

One day, I was sitting in the living room, and Sparky started to jump and snap at the air. She knocked over a vase of flowers on the coffee table. Annie came in to see what the ruckus was about.

"What's going on?" she exclaimed.

The answer was, "Sparky's chasing a fly."

When she was taken out, which I tried to do as little as possible, you never knew what she was going to do. Even with the shock collar, she would take off after a deer or a squirrel, and after disappearing into the woods, she might not make an appearance again for an hour. She collected rocks and enormous sticks, which she proudly deposited on the front porch as if they had great value. She was in constant motion.

"Daddy, Daddy," the kids said as they came bursting into the bedroom. "It snowed, it snowed!" Why are children constitutionally incapable of saying something only once? I looked out the window, and we had received about a half a foot of snow during the night.

"Looks like we'll have a white Christmas," said Annie, as it was three days before the holiday.

She got up and dressed to take the dog out. A few minutes later she was calling for me. I put on my robe and went downstairs. She was standing on the front porch, laughing. Out in the yard was Sparky, who was romping and rolling in the snow, which, it occurred to me, she had never seen before. I shook my head and it took Annie almost a half hour to get the dog to come back in.

The phone rang, and I answered it.

"Dr. McRae?"

"Yes," I said.

"This is Rachel Wise." She sounded distraught.

"Yes, Rachel, what's wrong?"

"I'm sorry to bother you at home, but there's something wrong with Tess."

She described the symptoms: high fever, cough, and headache.

"Rachel, you should take her to the hospital."

There was silence on the other end of the phone.

"Rachel?"

"Dr. McRae, I'm sorry to ask you this but would you look at her? I—I don't have any insurance."

The town of Evergreen was a small, close-knit community. Our major industry was Christmas. More precisely, Christmas trees, but the whole town traded on the nickname: Christmas Capital of the World. There were specialty stores that sold only Christmas-themed items, and at this time of year, people arrived from all over to drive up and down the streets to see the Christmas displays. There was hardly a yard without a nativity set, reindeer, Santa, inflatable snowmen, and, sometimes, all of them together.

I'm the only pediatrician in town. We have a small hospital that can take care of routine cases, but the more serious ones get transferred to the general hospital in the county seat.

I knew Rachel Wise. I knew practically everyone and, especially, if they had kids. Rachel's husband had been killed in an accident several years ago, leaving her with a daughter, Tess, who was now six. She worked at a local store as a clerk. It didn't surprise me that she didn't have insurance.

"Okay, Rachel, bring her to the office. I'll meet you there in fifteen minutes." I turned to go upstairs and tripped over the dog, who had stolen up behind me.

Rachel laid Tess on the exam table. The little girl was pale and sweaty. I took her vitals. Her temperature was 102.

"Rachel," I said, "Tess has some sort of an infection. I don't know what. She really needs to go to the hospital."

"But . . ." Rachel began to protest.

"Don't worry about the insurance," I said boldly. "We'll figure something out."

We drove to the hospital, and I carried Tess into the emergency room. I told the admitting nurse to find her a room, ordered some tests, and left with Tess in a bed and Rachel sitting by her side. I knew that Rachel would be there all night.

When I got home, it was dark, except for the Christmas lights on the house, but I could see something lying in the front yard. I parked the car and waded through the snow. There, lying in the snow, looking as angelic as could be, was the baby Jesus. Well, not *the* baby Jesus, but a statue of him.

"Sparky!" I said out loud.

"Annie!" I called, walking through the front door with the wooden baby in my arms. "Would you come here?"

"My goodness," she exclaimed, "where'd you get that?"

"On the front lawn. Did Sparky wander off again?"

"Yes," she said. "In fact, she's been gone for about thirty minutes. You don't think . . ."

"Annie, I know," I responded.

About ten minutes later, I heard scratching on the front door and opened it to find Sparky, tail wagging vigorously, with another baby Jesus in her mouth.

"Annie!" I yelled.

There are two schools of thought about manger scenes in Evergreen, and the topic is hotly debated. The community is divided into those who put the baby in the manger before Christmas and those who wait until Christmas Day. Growing up, we were Christmas Day people, and my brother and sister and I used to argue about who got to put Jesus in the manger on Christmas morning. When my parents died, I asked for the nativity scene, only to be told by my sister that she had sold it at a yard sale. I was pretty angry. It's not that I'm all that religious; it was just a piece of my childhood that was now gone.

I did love that nativity set and remembered that our baby Jesus was wooden and cherubic looking, in a blue blanket, and that one year my sister had dropped him and chipped off the end of his nose. Somehow, it didn't matter, though; it was still our Jesus.

Anyway, I realized that half the mangers in the neighborhood were already empty, waiting for Christmas, and there was no way to tell where these had come from.

After dinner, the doorbell rang. I went and looked through the window. It was someone delivering a package. I opened the door to sign for it, and Sparky was out the door like a bullet and disappeared down the street. By the time we caught her an hour later, we were in the possession of three more baby Jesuses—two plastic and one rather expensive-looking ceramic rendering.

"Good grief," I said to Annie, "what are we going to do now?"

The next morning, I drove to the hospital. It was snowing hard again, and the roads were not in good shape. I went up to Tess's room and found Bill Harper, one of the staff physicians; Tom McNabb, the local priest; and Rachel standing around the bed. We greeted each other.

"I've never seen anything like it," said Bill. "This fever won't break, and the tests haven't shown anything."

Bill and I consulted and decided to run some more tests. In other circumstances, I would have had her transferred to a larger hospital, but the weather wasn't going to permit that anytime soon.

Bill left, and I turned to leave, and then I could hear Rachel crying. "I don't know what I'm going to do," she sobbed.

Tom McNabb put his arm around her and motioned for me to come over, which I did.

"Now, Rachel," he said, "It's going to be all right. Jack here is an excellent doctor. He'll figure this out."

I wasn't so sure, but didn't say anything.

"How am I going to pay for this?" she said. "I don't have any insurance and this is getting more expensive."

Tom looked at me, but spoke to Rachel. "Don't worry about that, Rachel. We'll figure that out together. Why don't we pray?"

I've never been a big "prayer." I'm not against it; it's just that it's for other people, not for me. Tom laid one hand on Tess's forehead, took Rachel's hand with the other, and Rachel took mine. I went stiff, and it did not go unnoticed by Tom, who quickly launched into a prayer asking God to intervene. It seemed a little ridiculous to me. It seemed to go on forever, but finally he said, "Amen."

"Baby Jesus." The words had come from Tess, who hadn't spoken at all up until now.

"Baby Jesus," she said again, in a tone as if she were calling out to him.

"She's delirious," I said.

"Maybe, maybe not," said Tom, and then, "Rachel, I'm going to step out into the hall with Jack here. I need to talk with him."

Tom and I left the room.

"How serious is this, Jack?"

"Well, if we don't get the fever down soon, it could be very serious."

"Life threatening?"

I nodded, and then said, "I'm sorry about the insurance thing, but I didn't know what other options there were."

"Don't worry about that," said Tom. "God is faithful."

I must have looked dubious.

"Jack, I suspect that the whole faith thing is difficult for you, but God is just as real as your medicine. You do all you can, and God will take care of the rest."

"I just don't want to get her hopes up," I said.

"But that's what faith is," said Tom, "the evidence of things hoped for, the conviction of things not seen."

I wasn't sure, but I suspected he was quoting from the Bible.

I nodded again, and as I was walking away, he said, "Oh, Jack, I was talking with Faith Gunderson this morning, and she said she thought she saw your dog carrying a baby Jesus around town last night."

I was stunned, but said, "I'm sure she's mistaken."

When I got home that night, there were another eight baby Jesuses in the living room.

"Annie!" I exclaimed.

Annie came into the room. "I know, I know. She got away again and brought these back. Maybe we should call Chief Ellicott and tell him what's going on. I'm sure he's been receiving calls."

"I'll have to think about that," I said.

The phone rang. It was the hospital calling. There was a problem with Tess, and so I drove back over there.

When I got there, I discovered that Tess was in a coma. Rachel and Father Tom were there.

"This can't be good," Rachel sobbed.

I ordered some more tests and called a specialist I knew at another hospital.

I felt so helpless. Here was this woman, and all she had was her daughter, and she was trusting me to make her better, and not only could I not do that, but I didn't even know what was wrong, and she was getting worse.

"All we can do is wait and let the medicine do its job," I said.

"I think we should pray again," said Father Tom. He took a small bottle out of his pocket and poured a little oil on his thumb, made the sign of the cross on Tess's forehead, and we prayed again holding hands. I still wasn't comfortable with it.

When Tom finished we stood looking at the sick child, and she said, "Baby Jesus." I had heard of people talking while in a coma, but had never experienced it.

"See, it's a sign," said Tom.

"Can I see you in the hall?" I said.

When we were out of earshot from Rachel I said to him, "Father, I don't want you to give Rachel false hope."

"Why would I do that?" he replied.

"I mean that thing about the sign. You shouldn't say things like that."

"Why not? It is a sign."

"Tom, how do you know that?"

"Because I'm in the 'signs' business, that's how. Don't you believe in signs?"

"No, I don't," I said, and I walked away.

When I got home, Annie met me at the door.

"Now, Jack, don't be angry," she began, and I knew it had to be something about Sparky.

She took me to the living room, and I was astonished to see that we were now in the possession of twenty-eight baby Jesuses, spread all over the room.

"I don't believe this," I said.

"Tomorrow, I'm calling Chief Ellicott," Annie said. "We have to find who these belong to."

She went upstairs, but I was too distraught over Tess to sleep just yet. I made a cup of tea and sat down in the living room—me and twenty-eight baby Jesuses.

I began to think about the past several days. I had always been so competent at my work. Yes, I had had children die, but it was always because of circumstances beyond anyone's control. And in every one of those few cases, I at least knew what was wrong and what protocol to follow.

I thought about what it would be like to have one of my children in that situation, especially at Christmas. To not know if the next breath would be her last, to cling to some slim hope that a miracle would happen.

Some miracle would happen? Now I was sounding like Father Tom. But then I got to thinking about Christmas itself. I would go to church tomorrow night, Christmas Eve, and hear the story, and while I had some doubts about the details, I basically believed it was true. If God could send his son in the form of a baby and get shepherds and wise men to worship him, healing Tess would seem to be small in comparison.

And then I did something I hadn't done alone in a long time. I prayed. It wasn't long or elegant. I just said, "Lord, help me, heal Tess, and give me a sign." I felt my heart get warm and tears began to form in my eyes.

The doorbell rang.

This can't be good, I thought. I opened the door, and there was Father Tom. In one hand, he had Sparky by the collar, and in the other, he was holding another baby Jesus.

"This belong to you?" he asked, smiling and nodding toward the dog. I let him in. Tom stepped into the hallway, where he had a clear view of the living room and its new occupants. His eyes grew wide and he whistled. "Good grief. There's something you don't see every day."

I told him the story about how Sparky seemed to be hardwired to kidnap baby Jesus and that this had been going on for several days. I also told him we were calling Chief Ellicott in the morning.

He sat down in the living room and just stared. Then he looked over at me.

"Looks like you were crying," he said. "You okay?"

I almost said, "I'm fine," but then I shook my head "no" and another tear formed.

"What's wrong, Jack?"

And so I told him about what I had been thinking about, how helpless I felt, and how I had prayed.

"And what exactly did you pray for?" he asked.

"I asked him to help me, to heal Tess, and to give me a sign."

Tom was quiet for a moment and then:

"Jack," he said, "let me get this straight. You're asking God to give you a sign while you're sitting in a room filled with baby Jesuses? I think you got your sign."

I started to laugh one of those laughs mixed with tears.

"Jack," Tom said, "don't call Brian Ellicott tomorrow. I'll take care of this."

"What?"

"I'll take care of this, just trust me. Tomorrow, when you leave for the evening service, just leave all of these on the front porch." He got up to leave and before he went out he door, he said, "Oh, and one more thing . . ."

"What's that?"

"Buy Sparky a leash."

The next day I visited Tess on my rounds. She was no better. Rachel was becoming increasingly distraught, and I had nothing to offer her medically by the way of comfort. I was standing next to the bed looking at Tess, and I stretched out my hand, put it on her fevered forehead, and closed my eyes.

"Baby Jesus," she said.

"You know," said Rachel, "she only says that when you're in the room."

That night, before we went to church, we put all of the baby Jesuses on the front porch, like Tom had directed me.

At church, Tom preached about looking for the baby Jesus and wove in the story about Tess and how, even in her coma, she was looking for Jesus. He also let it be known that her hospitalization was going to be costly, and that Rachel didn't have any insurance.

After the sermon and the prayers and the peace it was time for the announcements. They were pretty typical except for the last one.

"It has come to my attention," Father Tom said, standing in the aisle, "that there has been a rash of baby Jesus thefts recently. I am pleased to announce that our own Jack McRae has recovered, we believe, all of them and that after the service, if yours is missing, you may go and reclaim it from his front porch." And then added, "Thank you, Jack."

I didn't know whether to smile proudly or crawl under the pew. God bless Tom McNabb, who made it sound like I had engaged in some nifty detective work instead of being the owner of the thief.

What I didn't know was that Tom had called all of the other ministers in town and told them that I had recovered the baby Jesuses, and asked them to make the same announcement. He also told them all about Tess.

After church, I felt like walking. So I piled Annie and the kids in the car and made my way through the snowy streets. I looked at the Christmas decorations in everyone's yard. I thought a lot about what we were celebrating, the birth of a child who would save the world. I thought about Tess and how Rachel was spending Christmas Eve in the hospital alone. It made me sad. I was wishing I knew what to do. It took me about thirty minutes to get home.

When I arrived, all but one of the Jesuses were gone from the porch. It looked like Father Tom's plan had been effective.

I picked up the remaining Jesus and held it in my arms as if it were real. I thought about Tess and wondered if there was any change. I looked into the baby's eyes. This one was wooden and cherubic looking, wrapped in a blue blanket, and then I noticed that the tip of his nose was broken off. And then I realized this one was mine, this was the baby Jesus we had growing up.

I was stunned, but suddenly, I knew what to do with this new sign.

I went to the car and put the baby Jesus on the seat next to me and drove to the hospital. If Tess wanted to see the baby Jesus, I would bring him to her.

I got off the elevator and turned the corner onto the hall where Tess's room was, and I couldn't believe my eyes. The hall was filled with dozens of different versions of baby Jesus. There must have been fifty or sixty of them. I walked into the room to discover that the reason they were in the hall was because the room was filled with them too.

Rachel and Father Tom were standing next to Tess's bed.

"Hello, Dr. McRae. Merry Christmas." The words were spoken by Tess, who was sitting up in bed, surrounded by images of the very thing she had been asking for in her illness: Jesus.

"Not you too," laughed Father Tom, pointing at the Jesus I had brought.

"What, what happened?" I said in disbelief.

"When the town heard the story about Tess, they apparently all had the same thought," said Tom. "They went home, or to your porch, got their baby Jesus, and brought it to the hospital for Tess. People have been coming all evening. About an hour ago, Tess's fever broke, and about fifteen minutes ago, she sat straight up in bed as if nothing had happened."

"It's a miracle," sobbed Rachel.

"And it gets better," said Tom, who was motioning to a stack of envelopes on a table. Everyone who came had brought a check to help with the medical expenses.

"I don't believe it," I said.

"Yes, you do," said Tom.

And he was right; I did believe. The story, of course, got out, and the next day the paper was there, and the story was picked up by the national wires. The picture of Tess surrounded by all of the Jesuses was too much to resist, and over the next weeks more money than she needed was sent to Rachel, who put the balance in a college fund for Tess.

I never did figure out what was wrong with Tess, and I guess it wasn't important. I did, however, figure out what was wrong with me. I had grown old and cold; I had stopped believing in the magic of miracles and the power of faith. I was the expert. But then I was confronted with the unsolvable, which drove me to my knees and into the arms of faith, into the arms of a baby who came to save the world.

2

LITTLE BROWN BATS AND SILLY VOICES

I'm told that clergy have an expression for some of their parishioners: "The C and E Gang." That stands for Christmas and Easter, referring to the folks who can't seem to find the church building fifty weeks a year, but never miss the two big holidays. I remember my father complaining when I was young that he couldn't get a seat on Easter morning because of "all these people I've never seen before." I think he actually had to repress the urge to ask whoever was occupying his preferred pew to please sit elsewhere.

I wonder whether clergy have an expression for people like me—I'll go to church anytime *except* Christmas.

This has nothing to do with the hypocrisy of the season, with crusty curmudgeons who suddenly catch the Christmas spirit like it's some sort of flu and turn all syrupy. And it has nothing to do with the story of Jesus's birth, hard to swallow though that may be. I'm fine with the angels and shepherds and wise men and the star and all that. I just don't want to have to deal with it all in person.

I mean, whose bright idea was it to stage "The Christmas Pageant"? The whole concept of it is ludicrous. As far as inventions go, it ranks up there with leisure suits, the Edsel, and bacon you can cook in the toaster: all incredibly bad ideas. I realize there may be nothing most people want to witness more than their six-year-old in an oversize bathrobe kneeling next to a box bearing a baby doll wrapped in a receiving blanket to portray Jesus. But not me; not anymore, anyway.

My first experience with a pageant was when I was six. I was cast as a shepherd. All I had to do was sit on the floor and watch as the angels came in. Then, when they finished singing "Angels we have heard on high," I was supposed to stand, point at them, and say, "Hark, a thrilling voice is sounding." One little line . . . one simple line. I practiced it for weeks. "Hark, a thrilling voice is sounding," over and over again. I wanted it to be perfect. I practiced various intonations and volumes until I got it just right, just perfect.

When the big night came, I was thrilled. I knew my line, I knew when to deliver it, and the pageant unfolded as planned. We shepherds entered, sat on the floor, the angels appeared, sang their song, and then . . . and then nothing. Ever see a kid playing right field in Little League sit down midgame and start to pick dandelions? That's what I did, essentially. I got completely lost in some thought, and when the angels finished, there was silence. Eventually the voice of Mrs. Murtland, the pageant director, delivering my cue, "Hark . . . Joe, Hark!" in a loud whisper, cut through my reverie. Realizing this was my big moment, I leapt to my feet and shouted, "Snark, a hilly voice is thounding."

Snark, a hilly voice is thounding? The congregation erupted into hysterics. I wanted to crawl away and die.

Then, when I was fourteen, I was asked to play my trumpet with the choir. Our choir director, Mr. Kaughman, had written this tremendous fanfare that would announce the arrival of the angels. I was good on the trumpet, so, despite my previous embarrassment, I accepted the role, mostly because I could more or less hide in the choir loft and not have to be in front of people. I practiced the piece for weeks; I would be perfect this time. I had it memorized. I played it flawlessly. On pageant night it came time for the angels to appear, the organ music rose, Mr. Kaughman pointed at me, and what emanated from my horn was later described as the sound of someone strangling a cat. I couldn't hit the high notes cold, I struggled to find my place, and the whole piece degenerated into cacophony. I finished what has to be the worst twelve-bar solo in the history of music, only to hear Mr. Kaughman say, "Okay, Joe, we're going to try that again." I was stupefied. The organ music came around again, I tried my solo again, but the results, if possible, were even worse. I spent the rest of the evening in tears.

But the worst was yet to come.

When I was sixteen, our church went through some sort of midlife crisis, which resulted in the leadership deciding that there weren't enough youth involved in significant moments of the church's life. They adopted the slogan "The youth is our future." They put teenagers on committees and assigned them to some jobs traditionally done by the adult members. It may have been a good idea in theory, but ultimately it didn't work very well. Most adults don't want to sit through three-hour meetings on Monday nights. What made them think a sixteen-year-old who just got a driver's license would want to?

It was during that time that Father Murtland approached me one day before Thanksgiving. "You know, Joe," he said to me in that deep, resonating voice of his, "we have embraced this wonderful new Youth Initiative."

"Uh-huh," I responded, leery of where this was going.

"And," he continued, "I was thinking that you would be the perfect person to organize and direct our Christmas pageant this year."

"Ah, well . . ."

"The script has already been selected and I have several adults who will help, but you'd make a fine director."

"Well, I um . . ."

"It would mean a great deal to me and the parish."

I hate that guilt thing grown-ups do to kids. The only place I had to go was, "Okay."

Father Murtland did have some good adults to help, as promised. But the burden for the production fell squarely on my shoulders. *I can do this*, I thought, *and this time it'll be perfect.*

"Why do you think Father Murtland asked you to direct the pageant?" my father asked me one evening as the event approached and I was feeling particularly anxious.

"Because no one else would do it," I responded unhelpfully.

"Possibly," he replied, choosing not to be angered by my sarcasm, "but I think it has more to do with your gifts."

"Yeah?"

"Yes. You're good with people, you do well in front of the public, you're a gifted musician, and you have some real leadership abilities."

Instead of being a comfort, the statement just added to my apprehension. "Dad, I don't see why I have to do this."

"Well, first of all, you said you would. But, more importantly, when God gives us a gift, he expects us to share it with others."

I've never been very good with the sharing thing.

The evening of the pageant, I was pretty strung out, but everyone seemed to know where they were supposed to be and what they were supposed to do. The church was packed.

The pageant started out well enough. Jack Clark did okay as John the Baptist, although his beard was coming loose so he kept pressing it back on, detracting from the drama of his prophetic utterances. There was some snickering in the congregation when the innkeeper, a tiny little guy whose name I forget, greeted the holy family with a "What do you want?" that was so hostile I thought Mary was going to burst into tears, but she and Joseph made it to the manger with the doll swaddled as Jesus.

The shepherds heard from the band of angels and they all arrived on cue at the manger, followed by the wise men, creating what I had envisioned as the perfect nativity tableau for the congregation to sing "Joy to the World."

Then it happened. Could someone please explain to me where, on a beautiful snowy December evening, a bat could possibly have come from?

Carol Mead saw it first as it swooped at the holy family like a dive-bomber, and she screamed as if she had been stabbed. The bat broke to the right just before the manger and everyone on that side screamed and either fell to the floor or ran to find their parents, and then complete chaos broke out. Joseph knocked the manger over, sending Jesus flying down the aisle. The bat came in for another pass and angels were falling over each other to get out of the way. Jimmy Byrd tripped over a wooden cutout of a sheep and arose from the floor with blood streaming from his nose, all over his white angel costume. The bat came by again. Now the grown-ups were into the act as parents rushed forward to try to get to their children, as if they were all in mortal danger. Mrs. Dempsey and Mrs. Landis got tangled up and fell in the aisle, and Mr. Mead fell over them, topped by several of the children who were already running at full speed toward them, causing a pileup like something from a surreal game of football. And still the bat was circling and still the children were screaming.

By a sheer act of will, and thanks to that deep, resounding voice, Father Murtland got everyone calmed down, and with the bat still performing its aeronautical stunts, managed to shepherd everyone downstairs to the parish hall, where the double door was shut firmly and actually locked, as if our flying antagonist might be able to open doors.

I watched the spectacle from the back of the sanctuary and when everyone had retreated downstairs I was left alone, in tears with a little brown bat circling the sanctuary.

The whole episode was humiliating enough in its own right, but the fact that I was left there alone, that no one knew I was missing, that I was locked out of being with everyone, all added insult to what was already more injurious than I could bear. I've never been back to a Christmas pageant again, and it's everything I can do to drag myself to any Christmas service, even though that was over fifteen years ago.

My father tried to console me after the catastrophe was over.

"Joe, there was nothing you could have done to have stopped it."

Just the mention of "it" brought me to tears.

"I wanted it to be perfect," I managed.

"I know," my father said. "But you gave your best."

"My 'best' was a riot that landed three kids in the emergency room . . . and Mr. Mead is still limping," I whined.

"Joe, all God wants from us is our best; it's never perfect, but it is good enough. When we give him our best, the results are secondary. What's important is . . ."

"I know," I interrupted. "I tried."

"No, Joe. What's important is that you gave God your best, and I'm proud of you," he said wisely

Now I was crying again.

Since that time, I have gone to college, have a nice position in a legal firm, and have been married. But the pain of the "Night of the Christmas Bat," as it became known in the parish, never left. I've only told the story once before now, to my wife, maybe five years ago.

We had just sat down for dinner and I was about to try the beautiful casserole my wife had created when she said, "Joe, Father Donaldson called today."

She had that tone in her voice like she knew I wasn't going to like what was coming next. My chest tightened.

"Now, don't be angry but he'd like Samuel to be in the Christmas pageant."

Samuel was our first and only child, just two months old. The only possible role he could play in the pageant was Jesus.

There was a long silence.

It was inconceivable to me that, after all I had been through, Kate would expect me to allow our perfect little boy to be in a pageant.

"Joe," she finally said, "you need to get over your fear. Whether it's this year or ten years from now, you know Samuel is going to want to be in the pageant."

"No," I said quietly.

We ate dinner in silence.

The next Sunday after church, Father Donaldson stopped me. "Kate told me you don't want Samuel to be in the pageant."

I was a little embarrassed.

"I hope you'll reconsider. Samuel is the only child young enough to fill the role."

"Why not use a doll?" I offered.

"Well, that's what we'll have to do, I suppose, but that would be too bad because the tradition in this parish is that the youngest child plays Jesus. Most parents consider it a privilege. One couple a few years back actually tried to plan their pregnancy so their baby could be Jesus! Will you give it a little more consideration?"

I told him I would.

"What if something happened?" I said to Kate, when she worked up enough courage to broach the subject with me again.

"Joe, be reasonable. There are thousands of church Christmas pageants every year and no one gets hurt."

"That's what you think."

"Joe, listen, Emily Masters has been cast as Mary. She's practically an adult, she babysits all over town, she knows what she's doing, and we'll be right there."

"Kate, we'd feel awful if something terrible happened."

"Joe, let's be honest. Something terrible could happen at any minute anywhere, but we can't live paralyzed by the fear of that."

"I don't find that thought comforting."

"It's not about your comfort. It's about doing what's best."

"I don't think I can."

"Now at least you're being honest," she said. "This isn't really about baby Samuel; this is about a sixteen-year-old boy looking for perfection, then being left alone after the most embarrassing moment of his life. Joe, it's time you stopped being that person."

"Why?" was my brilliant retort.

"Because if you stay stuck there, you cannot be your best and you cannot give your best to God."

I knew she was right.

"Joe, who are you angry with?"

"I'm not mad at anyone," I snarled. But it didn't feel that way.

"Yes, you are. And once you figure that out, you won't be stuck any more."

I had trouble falling asleep that night. All sorts of images were flying through my head. I could see children running and shrieking, and Father Murtland corralling people out of the sanctuary and down the stairs. I could see the congregation laughing at me, and Mr. Kaughman saying, "We're going to try this again." I thought about Kate telling me I was angry and needed to get "unstuck." But the last thing I remember before falling asleep was my father saying, "What's important is to give God your best."

"Joe. Joe, wake up! Something terrible has happened."

My wife was jostling me with a frantic motion. "Joe, something's wrong with Samuel."

I hurried down the hall to the baby's room. Kate had taken Samuel from the crib. He was motionless.

"Listen," said Kate. And then I could hear a heavy rasping sound coming from Samuel. It was his breathing. "Joe, I can't get him awake and he's burning up."

I threw on some clothes and rushed to the car. Kate dressed and we drove—like the proverbial bat out of you-know-where—to the hospital.

There is nothing worse than having a sick child and not knowing what's going on. I felt utterly helpless and unsure of myself. All I knew was that it felt like the most important thing in my life was about to be taken away from me. It has been said that there are no atheists in foxholes; surely the same is true for parents with sick children. Driving to the emergency room, I found myself praying, trying to bargain with God, telling him that if he'd let Samuel live I would do anything he asked. Only later did I realize that this was the first time I had really, truly prayed in years.

The emergency room wasn't busy. We were taken into a curtained area immediately and a doctor came in. She introduced herself and, after a few preliminary questions, began her exam.

"Well, we won't know for sure until we get some test results back, but this sounds like pneumonia. We're going to have to admit Samuel." The staff started him on IV antibiotics and something to keep him from getting dehydrated, and several hours later we found ourselves in a hospital room.

I don't think I've ever seen anything as heartbreaking as my infant son hooked up with plastic lines in his arm all covered with gauze, breathing with difficulty. He seemed so small, so alone, and so vulnerable. I would do anything for him.

"How are you doing, Joe?" I looked up to see Father Donaldson. It was so unlike me, but I leapt up and just put my arms around him and began to cry.

"It's okay, Joe," he said. "You're not alone. We're going to take this walk together."

"I'm so scared," I said.

"Well, it's a scary time, but it will pass. God does not abandon his children." Father Donaldson prayed for Samuel and for us. Although I don't remember his words, it felt like a burden was lifting.

Kate collapsed in a chair and fell asleep. Father Donaldson said, "Let's stretch our legs. Kate's right here and Samuel is in good hands. You need a little change of scenery."

We left the room and roamed the halls of the hospital in silence. Finally, Father Donaldson opened a door and motioned for me to go in.

I didn't realize that hospitals actually had real chapels. This one even had little pews. I sat down in one and the old priest sat down in the one in front of me and turned around.

"So, what did you promise God?" he asked.

"Promise God?" I repeated.

"On your way over here, or since you got here—what did you promise God?"

I was exhausted. "I promised him I'd do anything."

"What does that mean?"

"It means that Samuel is more important to me than anything else, and that I would do anything to . . ." I began to choke up.

Father Donaldson let the moment hang and then said, "Anything to . . . what?"

"Anything to keep him from dying."

"What could you possibly do for God?" he asked.

"What could I do for God?"

"Yes. What could you do that God can't?"

"Well, God can do anything, can't he?" I wondered aloud.

"Well, pretty much, but if you're going to bargain with God, you must have something he wants."

"Have something God wants?" Now I was really stumped. "I don't know."

"Well, you'll figure it out, and when you do you'll get unstuck, son. I'm going to go now."

The old priest left me alone in the chapel.

The next day the doctor visited and confirmed her initial diagnosis. Samuel had pneumonia and another respiratory infection as well. It was serious, but she felt certain that it wasn't life threatening.

A couple of days passed, and Samuel showed great improvement. The doctor anticipated discharging him later that day. I had taken a late lunch and left work early to get to the hospital. Kate hadn't eaten, so I sent her to the cafeteria and I stayed with Samuel. He was off his tubes, lying peacefully in my arms. He looked perfect.

It was very quiet, and I found myself replaying the events and conversations of the past week.

I was angry; Father Donaldson had been right about that. But angry at whom? And both Kate and Father Donaldson had told me I needed to get unstuck, and I certainly did feel stuck, but I didn't know why. And then there was Father Donaldson's haunting question about what I had that God might want.

What is it that I have that God wants? I thought. *What can I possibly give to God?* And then I prayed again.

"Okay, God," I said, looking into my son's face. "I know I promised you that if Samuel was okay I'd do anything. But you're going to have to tell me what you want." I even concluded with, "Amen." I held Samuel close, and kissed his forehead. I closed my eyes and gave thanks.

The door to Samuel's hospital room swung open, and I was surprised to see a little boy of about six standing there. Oddly, he was dressed like a shepherd, headdress and all.

"Hi," he said nonchalantly.

"Hello," I said.

"What's wrong with him?" he asked, pointing at Samuel.

"He's sick," I said.

"Is he going to die?"

"No, he's not. He's getting better."

"My brother's sick, too."

"Oh, I'm sorry," I said, too cowardly to ask the question he had asked. "What's you name?"

"Nathan! Nathan Edgar Martinson, the Third," he said, very proudly, as though I should know that.

Then I recognized him. He was Ed Martinson's kid from church.

"Lose your sheep?" I offered.

"Huh?"

"You look like a shepherd, so I thought you might be looking for your sheep."

He stood there quietly, his face growing somber, and a tear ran down his face.

I stood up. Carrying Samuel, I went over to Nathan. "I'm sorry," I said.

"I'm supposed to be in the Christmas Pageant," he said, "but Billy's sick and Mom says we can't go now."

"I'm sorry," I said, again.

"And I've practiced my line for weeks, and now I won't get to do it!"

I didn't know what to say. There was a moment of awkward silence and then Nathan's countenance changed.

"Want to hear it?" he asked hopefully.

I paused for just a second. "Of course," I managed.

His face brightened. "Now, you sit over there." He motioned toward the chair. Obediently, I sat down.

He knelt on the floor in front of the door, and looked across the room at the ceiling. After a few moments' intent concentration, he rose to his feet, pointed up at some imagined object, and shouted, "Hark, a silly voice is sounding!"

Nathan turned to me, took a deep bow, and grinned from ear to ear.

Beaming, he said, "I gave it my best."

"That was perfect," I said, and the word *perfect* hung in the air like a cloud.

I was looking at this little boy, dressed like a shepherd, who wanted to do his best, gave it his all, but got it wrong; then at Samuel, my perfect little child, who'd been so sick I could have lost him. And then I was looking back at a sixteen-year-old boy who had done his best, but didn't consider it good enough, though it was good enough for God.

And I think I understood grace. That God takes us as we are, imperfect and flawed, and touches our lives and says, "I know you're not going to get this right all of the time, but that's okay. Because my love is greater than your shortcomings. And there's nothing you can do to make me love you any less."

And suddenly I knew what it was that God wanted from me.

"You okay, mister?" I was crying now, and Nathan scrambled over and gave me and Samuel a big hug. "It's okay," he said. "He's going to be okay."

"Whatever is all this?" It was Kate in the doorway, witnessing quite a sight: her husband sitting in a rocker with their infant son, both being hugged by a diminutive shepherd.

"Well, hello, Nathan," said Kate.

And then she leaned out the doorway and said, "Marcie, he's in here." In short order, Nathan's mom appeared in the room.

"Oh, Joe, I'm sorry he's in here bothering you. I was scared to death Nathan had run off; he wants to be in that pageant so desperately."

"How's Billy?" I asked.

"He'll be fine, thankfully; but we'll be spending the evening in the hospital. Nathan will just have to wait 'til next year."

The nurse appeared in the doorway. "Paperwork's all done and Samuel is ready to be discharged; if you'll sign, you folks can go home now."

"Can we take him?" I asked.

"Of course we can take him," said Kate. "That's what the nurse just said."

"No, I mean Nathan," I explained.

"Joe?" said Kate. "What are you saying?"

"I mean, can we take Nathan to the pageant for you, Marcie?"

"Oh, I couldn't ask you to do that. . . ."

"Oh, please, Mommy. Please, please, pul-ease!"

"It would mean a great deal to me," I said.

Kate looked at me, incredulous.

We arrived at church late and the pageant was already under way. We stood in the back and I wasn't sure what to do. The shepherds were all seated and the heavenly host were singing. We were going to miss Nathan's part!

But Nathan was not to be denied. As the last "in excelsis deo" faded away, Nathan, still standing beside me, shouted at the top of his lungs, "Hark, a silly voice is sounding!" Everything stopped and the whole world seemed to be moving in slow motion. A stunned congregation turned to see who it was, and once more I found myself on the verge of a nativity catastrophe. But this time somehow I knew what to do.

Carrying Samuel, I took Nathan's hand and we walked up the aisle. When we got to the manger, Nathan took a bow and went to his place, and I . . . I handed Samuel to Mary, who took him ever so maternally and gently placed him in the manger.

What did God want? What was it that he didn't have? What he didn't have was me. And as long as I held on to Samuel, or on to my expectations for perfection, as long as I held onto my anger for my shortcomings, he wasn't going to have me. So I gave it all to him that night, the good stuff that I was proud of, along with the bad stuff that made me crazy. And to my amazement, he took it. He took it all, and I tell you, I felt him hold me in his arms as gently and tenderly as a mother holds her newborn babe.

3

ANGELS UNAWARE

I can't find the mail. I know it's here somewhere, just never in its designated place on any given day. I come home from the office and the first thing I ask is, "Did we get any mail today?" The answer is always the same: "Yes." Then I say, "Where is it?" Then follows a long pause, after which my wife replies, "Well, it's here somewhere."

At about that point, I give up. Not that there's ever any mail for me anyway. It's all bills, and junk mail, and periodicals for my wife and the kids. But it's the thought of this disorder—it drives me crazy. Why can't things be more orderly? It doesn't take any more time to do things right.

Take my kids, for instance. Four of them, all old enough to know how to wash a dish or pick up dirty clothes, but would they ever do so on their own? No, sir! You'd think that after a pair of underwear had hung on the bedpost for a week someone would grow tired of looking at it and toss it down the laundry chute.

All I want is a little order in my life, the operative word being "little." The lack of order is a great frustration to me.

Eight-year-old Leslie is our youngest child, and a handful; *precocious* is the word that comes to mind. When she was five, she once told the mailman that her parents had gone away to Austria and left her alone, thus occasioning a brief and rather humorless visit from the local police to ascertain the veracity of the fable.

One night near Christmas, I was tucking her into bed, praying along silently as she offered her intercessions. ". . . and God bless Mommy and Daddy, and Aunt Vera and Uncle Scott and Angel and Grandpa . . ."

"Who's Angel?" I asked.

"Hush, Daddy, I'm praying," she scolded.

"Sorry," I offered, and let her finish her litany entailing each of the girls in her class and Hannah Thomas's gerbil.

"Amen," she said finally.

"Now," I began again, "who is Angel?"

"Oh, no one," she said in a coy, singsongy tone.

"Leslie Grace!" I said, only feigning anger.

"Okay," she said, with a sigh. "Angel is the dog."

"What dog?" I asked, clueless.

"The dog Santa's bringing me."

"I thought you didn't believe in Santa anymore."

"Honestly, Dad, why don't you just ruin your youngest child's Christmas?"

"Are we talking about 'no Santa' or the dog?"

"Well, if *you* won't get me a dog, I guess I'll have to believe in *Santa*."

"You'd better believe real hard," I retorted.

"Dad, if you're not careful, I'm going to grow up warped."

"Good!" I said, kissing her forehead. "Then you'll be just like the rest of us."

I went into the living room. *Just what we need*, I thought, *a dog*. I shuddered at the thought of the chaos *that* would bring into the house. Muddy carpets, fur on the furniture, and clumps of the stuff rolling along, gathering dust on the hardwood floors in the hallways. And they drool!

Susie, my wife, came in and sat down. "So," she began, in a way that let me know that what was coming next had a certain amount of controversy attached to it. "Do you know what the kids want for Christmas?"

"The baby tells me she wants a dog," I said, using that not-in-*my*-lifetime tone.

"John, Leslie is no baby, and I think it would be wonderful to have a dog."

"Have you lost your mind? It's all we can do to keep a modicum of order around this house as it is. A dog is only going to make it worse."

"It'll teach the children responsibility."

"Susie, our kids won't finish the last inch of water in the water pitcher because they don't want to have to refill it. I don't believe a dog is going to help."

"Please, John. Think about it." She made those big doe eyes at me and playfully stuck out her bottom lip like a hurt child.

"Susan," I asserted, "it's not a good idea."

The next day was my weekly basketball game at the Y. Afterward I was nursing my wounds in the locker room and Billy Nash sat down next to me. He and his wife are in the same Bible study as we are at church.

"Can you believe that Porter guy?" he said with disgust. "I guess he never heard of three seconds in the paint."

"Yeah," I said distractedly.

"What's wrong with you today?" he asked. "You're not your naturally cheery self." He gave me that ironic smile of his.

"The family wants a dog."

"Oh, dogs are great!" Billy said.

"Not you, too," I groaned. "It's a conspiracy."

"What? Don't you like dogs?"

"I like dogs in the abstract, but not in the concrete."

"What, allergic to them?"

"No, it's the mess they make, all the work they require. It'll be just more chaos."

"Yeah, but that's part of what makes them great to have around."

"I beg your pardon?"

"I think that one of the reasons we have dogs is to increase our faith."

"You've lost me."

"Look at the world from God's point of view. What are you to God?"

"Uh . . ."

"You're a complete mess."

"Well, thanks a lot!"

"Not just you, it's all of us. We're all far too much work and bother. We're always messing things up and being where we shouldn't be. And yet God continues to care for us."

"Great, so now I'm God's dog."

"It's an analogy, John. Let me put it this way. You're right; dogs are a pain for us. They're difficult, just like we are to God."

"Then, why does God bother to put up with us?"

"DING! We have a winner!" shouted Billy in his "announcer" voice. "That's precisely the question, John. Why does God put up with us? What would possess the Creator of the universe not only to care for us but to pay the price for our sins?"

"I don't know."

"Yes, you do," he said, and left to take his shower.

But I didn't know. It was bad enough that I was being pressured to get a dog for Christmas on emotional grounds, but now I was getting theological pressure as well.

That evening Susie took the kids out to do some Christmas shopping, and I was left alone in the house. The sun had set and the house was quiet. Peaceful. I had just settled into my favorite chair with a cup of tea and a good book when I heard a sound at the front door. A little burst of winter's wind must've blown something against the door. Nothing of significance. I ignored it.

Then it happened again, but louder, and like a rough brushing or scratching sound. Odd. I went to the front door, flicked on the porch light, and looked out the window at the top of the door, but there was no one there. I turned off the light and started back to my chair, only to hear it again. I reeled around, flipped the light back on, and flung open the door.

There, sitting expectantly on the porch, was a dog. A big black cocker spaniel.

He sat, and I stood, and we stared at each other through the glass of the storm door.

"What?" I said, and he cocked his head to one side, a big floppy ear nearly touching the ground. Then he gently pawed the glass.

"Go on, shoo!" I yelled, but he just cocked his head to the other side and lifted his paw again.

I opened the door a bit, intending to be more menacing, but he stuck his snout into the opening and pushed right past me into the house.

"Hey! Just where do you think you're going?"

He paused, turning as if to reply, his little bobbed stub of a tail wiggling excitedly. Then he trotted off down the hall.

"Oh no you don't," I barked, and followed after him into the living room in time to see him relieve himself on the Christmas tree. I was stunned. This is exactly what I was talking about! Nothing but trouble.

"Scram!" I bellowed. I lunged for the animal, grabbing hold of his collar. He pulled back, slipping out of the collar, and scampered back out into the hall. The storm door slammed shut just as I reached the entry. He had pushed the unlatched door open and run off. I stepped to the end of the porch and proceeded down the front walk, looking up and down the street, but saw no sign of the culprit. Steamed, I went back inside and cleaned up the mess.

Later that night, Susie awakened me, as I had fallen asleep reading in my chair. "John. John. Honey," she whispered. "Wake up."

"I'm awake," I lied.

She stood staring at me for a moment, and then asked gently, "Can you tell me why there's a dog collar here on the coffee table?"

"Huh?"

"A purple dog collar. *Bethlehem Animal Shelter* is written on it."

We knew of the Bethlehem Animal Shelter; it was about five miles away in a part of town I don't often frequent. I checked the address in the phone book and wandered over there the next afternoon. I was greeted in the reception area by a pleasant young woman in a white lab coat. She introduced herself as Lillian.

"Do you have a black cocker spaniel?" I asked

Her face brightened and she practically sang, "Why, yes, this is your lucky day. Follow me!"

All I wanted to do was tell her to keep a better watch on her animals, but she opened a door and headed down a hall, and I had no choice now but to follow.

The room we entered was filled with perhaps seventy cages stacked two or three high, each with a dog peering expectantly through the bars. Pugs, poodles, sheepdogs, shepherds, and lots of mutts. Lillian was at the far end of the room opening a cage. She took out its contents, and the black cocker spaniel who'd visited me the night before came bounding down the corridor. He was all wiggles and ears and glossy black fur, and when he reached me he jumped up, putting his front paws on my thighs, and panting excitedly. His breath smelled like garbage.

"How's that one?" she asked triumphantly.

"Well, it might be him," I said. "I only saw him for a few minutes."

"He's yours?"

"Oh no, he's not mine," I said emphatically, and then I told her about the previous night's episode.

"Well, that's impossible," she protested. "There's no way the dogs can get out, and, as you've said, you live five miles away."

"Well, then, explain this," I said, producing the collar bearing the shelter's name.

Lillian was momentarily stunned. She looked at me and then at the dog, and then back at me. "Well, do you want him? He's really a great dog, a gorgeous glossy English cocker. People pay a small fortune for this breed, and most of the time they don't end up with a companion half this glorious."

"Do I want him? Are you mad? Why would I want him?" I blurted, pushing the dog away. Undeterred, he lay down at my feet, setting one chubby paw right on top of my shoe. His little stump of a tail wagged wildly, causing his whole back end to wiggle. He was comical, I'll concede that.

"Look at him," she cooed. "He's a baby doll. All he needs is a good home and someone to love him."

Without moving his head, the dog looked up at me, his droopy big brown eyes pleading.

"It's not a good idea," I said. The line came naturally; I had certainly rehearsed it enough.

"I get fifteen to twenty-some dogs a month, all unwanted for one reason or another. I keep them all here until I can find them a home. You'd be surprised at how many people are heartless toward animals," she said, her tone slightly accusing.

I chose to remain silent, and continued to look at the mass of black fur at my feet. The thing rolled over on its back, hoping to have his stomach scratched.

"It's why I called this place *Bethlehem*. You know, Jesus was homeless, too."

"Yes," I said, "but he didn't relieve himself on my Christmas tree."

Later that afternoon I was back at home, reviewing the day's mail in my favorite chair. Billy's words, about how God loves us even when we don't deserve it and how he paid for our sins so that we might live, kept repeating in my mind. There was a connection between that and this dog.

Then I heard a noise. I held my breath. Something was on the porch. Instinctively I knew what it was.

Then the doorbell rang.

If that dog is ringing my doorbell, I thought, *I'm either going to have to keep it or get myself a psychiatrist.*

The bell rang again. I got up and opened the door. There stood Sam Cooper from across the street. I smiled, relieved. "Hey, Sam," I said. Then I saw, tucked under his arm, a dog. A black cocker spaniel.

"Hey, John. May I come in?"

"Yes, yes, of course," I stammered, and Sam stepped just inside the door and set the dog down. Immediately the critter slipped around behind me as if hiding, and peered cautiously around my legs at Sam.

"I didn't know you had a dog," Sam started.

"We don't have a dog," I said.

"Well, he sure looks like yours, and when I found him digging up my rosebushes and chased him, he came right here."

"Sam, this is not my dog."

"It's all right, John," he said. "The damage is minimal. Just keep a better eye on him. That's all I'm asking. He's a very handsome animal; just a little spirited, that's all."

"Sam . . ."

"Say no more," he said. "Have a Merry Christmas!" He darted out the door and down the steps.

I wasn't sure whether to be glad that Sam had been so gracious or upset that he'd blamed me for what had happened.

I turned to glare at the culprit, but he wasn't there. *Great*, I thought.

I started to search the house. I found him pretty quickly. He would have been hard to miss, standing there on the middle of the dining room table, eating joyously out of a box of Godiva chocolates that Susie had received as an early Christmas present.

What greater proof did I need that having a dog was not a good idea?

I put him in the car and drove him to the shelter.

"You fed him chocolate?!" exclaimed Lillian. "Don't you know how bad that is for a dog?"

"I did *not* feed him chocolate," I protested. "He climbed up onto the table and helped himself! Besides, what's he doing out again, anyway?"

"It happens," she said dismissively. "The cage was being cleaned."

"You should take better care of him," I pressed.

"Nice of you to care," she said. "When did you become Albert Schweitzer, Mr. Tenderheart?" A tear rolled down her cheek. She looked dog tired, I realized, not intending the pun.

"Look," I said. "I'm sorry."

"No, you're not," she sniveled. "You don't care at all. Please leave."

And I did.

I found myself in a sour mood driving home. I had an uneasy feeling that I was somehow conspiring against providence, as if I weren't quite getting the message. I had told Susie none of this, except for the incident the first night, because I knew what she would say: "See, John, it must be God's will."

That night I was saying prayers with Leslie again. She was still praying for Angel, the dog she wouldn't be getting. I decided not to pursue the matter with her. I bent over to give her a hug and a kiss good night, slipped my hand under the pillow, and felt paper.

"What's this?" I asked, pulling it out.

"That's a picture of Angel. I tore the page out of a magazine," she responded.

"When?"

"Thanksgiving."

"Oh," I said, and opened the folded magazine page to see a color photo of a black English cocker spaniel. "Ohh."

I left the room, picture in hand.

I went to the living room and collapsed in my favorite chair. I stared at the picture a long time, incredulous.

"Whatcha got there?" Susie asked, coming into the room.

I handed her the magazine page.

"What's this?"

"It's the dog Leslie wants."

"Aww . . . what a beauty. Oh! Isn't this like the dog you said was here the other night?"

"Precisely." I took a deep breath. "Susie, I need to tell you something."

"John," she exclaimed when I finished telling her about the incidents at the shelter and with our neighbor Sam. "These are messages from God!"

"I knew you'd say that."

"Well, how else do you explain it all?"

I couldn't.

She picked up her purse and went to the front closet.

"What are you doing?" I asked.

"I'm grabbing my coat." She tossed mine at me. "We're going to that shelter and getting that dog."

"Susie, it's nearly nine at night! Can't this wait until tomorrow?"

She was already out the door. I followed after her.

Snow began to fall in big tender flakes as we drove in silence to the Bethlehem Animal Shelter.

There was a light on at the shelter when we arrived. After a wait of several minutes in the brisk air, the door was finally answered. Lillian recognized me immediately.

"What do you want at this hour?" she asked coolly. "The shelter's closed. I'm just finishing up some paperwork."

"We've come for Angel," said Susie, cheerily.

"Angel?" questioned Lillian, ushering us inside, and Susie spilled out the whole story.

Lillian listened intently. Then she said quietly, "He's not here."

"Not here!"

"No. He's disappeared again and I can't find him anywhere."

I was oddly disappointed. I felt almost as though I had lost something.

On the drive home, we were silent. As we turned up the road into our neighborhood, I found myself saying, "Maybe we should drive around a while and see if we can find him."

We cruised around the neighborhood, but saw nothing. The snowfall was pretty, and the roads were now blanketed, so we returned home, defeated.

Susie went to check on the children and I sat back down in my chair. Why did I feel this way? This creature . . . this dog . . . was really a big problem. Every encounter I had had with it was disastrous. It messed in the house, dug up the neighbor's bushes, stood on our dining room table. There was no earthly reason to be attached to this animal. Why did I care?

I could hear Billy saying in the locker room, "Why does God care? You know why."

And then I heard the noise at the door. I sat motionless, in case I had imagined it. "Susie," I called gravely. She came running.

"I think I heard something."

We went to the door together and opened it carefully. Nothing was there, but a circle of paw prints had been left in the snow.

"It's got to be him!" said my wife.

I stepped out and could see the paw prints winding across the front yard and out into the unplowed street. Snow hadn't been forecasted, but now I was grateful for the fresh snowfall, as it provided a crisp trail for me to follow. Without stopping to don coat or boots, I dashed out to follow the tracks. They led me down the street and into Mrs. O'Reilly's yard four doors away, and up onto her porch.

Mrs. O'Reilly was a delightful elderly widow who had taken a liking to the children. They'd gather frequently on her porch for tea and sympathy, and she allowed them one Tums tablet per visit. She occasionally came over for dinner, and we would help her with little chores like shoveling snow and such.

Given the weather and the hour, I was surprised to find Mrs. O'Reilly's heavy front door slightly ajar. As I reached for the doorbell, I heard a crash and a shriek. A light flashed, and through the high window of the door, I saw Mrs. O'Reilly's silver curls bobbing down the hallway. She was shouting harshly, clearly in distress. Dispensing with formality, I pushed open the door and headed after her down the hall.

The house was in complete motion. A lamp had been toppled, area rugs were askew, and a cacophony of hissing and barking and galloping sounds escalated. There was a clatter, as of a stack of china breaking. In a heartbeat, Mrs. O'Reilly's long-haired gray cat, Dustbunny, shot past me into another room, screeching in terror, followed closely by the tabby, the calico, and, right on their heels . . . a black cocker spaniel. The dog hit the brakes when he saw me, and the little hall rug he tried to stop on carried him like a genie on a magic carpet right to my feet, where he promptly sat, his stump of a tail wagging with delight. There was the soft chorus of twelve cat paws skittering across linoleum back in the kitchen. Then all fell silent.

"Mrs. O'Reilly," I called, not taking my eyes off the dog. "Mrs. O, are you all right?"

Mrs. O'Reilly emerged from the kitchen, breathless, wielding a broom. Her usually immaculate coif was tousled into random wisps and waves.

"Oh, John, thank goodness!" she huffed. "Am I glad to see you!"

"You okay?" I asked.

"I think so," she panted. "I found this dog on my porch and foolishly opened the door, only to have him come scampering in and start chasing the cats . . . and then . . . why, just look at this mess!"

"It's all right now," I said, offering her a hug and a comforting pat on the shoulder. "I think everything's settled down now."

Mrs. O'Reilly leaned the broom against the doorway and looked at the dog. "When I find the owner of this creature, I'm going to give him a piece of my mind!"

The dog nudged my leg, and pleaded at me with his big brown eyes. He panted softly, his pink tongue hanging out. A long strand of drool dripped onto my shoe.

I looked at Mrs. O'Reilly, then at the dog, and then back at dear, angry Mrs. O'Reilly. And then I surprised myself, saying, "He's mine. I am so very sorry for the mess and so very sorry for upsetting you and the cats. Please forgive me. You have my assurance that I will make all of this right. The dog belongs to me."

"John," came the voice softly. But Mrs. O'Reilly hadn't moved her lips. The voice had come from behind me. I turned to see Susie, who had apparently arrived in time to hear my little speech.

Then I had a strange experience. Everything went silent and stopped, and for just a moment I think I saw the world the way God does. I saw the mess of my own home and my own life: the way that I chase after stuff that is so destructive, and the ruin that I leave in my path. I'm certain I heard another soft voice, a deeper voice of unmistakable love and authority, saying, "I'll take care of it, I'll make it right. He belongs to me."

"John," whispered Susie. "Are you okay? You're crying."

Needless to say, Angel never went back to the shelter. Mrs. O'Reilly was gracious and forgiving, marveling as we told her the story of how we came to have this dog. We put her house back together and offered to replace the broken china, and the cats eventually reemerged, unscathed.

The next night was Christmas Eve, and we left Angel sleeping on the couch in the family room when we went to Midnight Mass. As I sat in the pew that night and heard the familiar story of the angels and wise men, of the holy family homeless and poor, my mind drifted back to the events of the previous several days. I knew I still wouldn't ever be able to find the mail and that there would still be clothes strewn all over the kids' bedrooms. I also knew that this dog was only going to add to the jumble.

But the connection between all this chaos and Christmas itself was becoming clearer to me. Why in the world would I compensate for the damages of a stray dog? Why would I care? My basketball buddy Billy was right; I did know the answer. And the answer was this: God bothers with us because he loves us unconditionally, and designed us in his image, with an amazing capacity to love, imperfect though we are in exercising that love.

This baby whose birth we were celebrating that night is God incarnate. His powerful, perfect love reaches into the chaos I create, pays for the damages I inflict, and redeems my brokenness, undeserving though I am of such amazing love. And with that, he gives me the capacity to love and forgive likewise. By paying for the chaos I've created, he has made me anew, given me a fresh start, and, thanks to this truth brought home to me by a stray dog, my life will never again be the same.

4

LITTLE MISS CHRISTMAS TREE

This is a story about the best Christmas I ever had. The Christmas I gave it all away.

I grew up in a small town. One of those places with a beautiful town square that has a gazebo where people go to be married because it is so picturesque. Looking back on it now, it was a great place to grow up. We knew the shopkeepers and the police, and even though I chaffed under the smallness sometimes, I can't think of any other place I'd rather have spent my childhood.

Our little town was supported by one and only one industry: Christmas tree farms. Within twenty miles of town there were no fewer than twelve different farms. In fact, no county in the country produced more Christmas trees than ours did; they even called the town and the county "Evergreen."

It's not unusual for small towns to have some type of scholarship pageant. There's a town in the next county that has the "Miss Dairy Maid" pageant, which celebrates the local milk farmers, and I heard of another one called the "Miss Goat Cheese" pageant. I'm not sure there's a scholarship big enough for that "honor." Our town was no different, and the most anticipated event of the year happened the weekend before Christmas. It was the "Little Miss Christmas Tree" pageant. I'm not sure why it was the "Little" Miss, because you had to be a senior in high school to compete.

The incentive for entering, besides the local honor, was a $5,000 college scholarship. So every year, twenty to thirty girls competed for the honor of being "Little Miss Christmas Tree."

Of course, in a small town, decorum is everything, so there was no swimsuit competition. But the girls were judged on academics, poise, appearance, talent, and an interview. The academics were submitted on the application, a lengthy interview was conducted the afternoon of the pageant, and Saturday night was the show where the girls were introduced, performed their talent, and answered one question chosen at random from a red Santa hat. The winner was announced and was crowned by last year's winner with a wreath of evergreen. Only the winner got a crown. Beauty was supposed to count for only 10 percent, but only the prettiest girls ever participated.

The competition was fierce, and in utter defiance of the spirit of Christmas, dirty tricks were not uncommon. One year Megan Conner couldn't find her shoes before she went onstage. Another year Erin Johnson found her baton (her talent was twirling) had been covered with maple syrup, and on still another occasion, Rebecca Michelson got locked in the bathroom just before she was to perform.

The best one, though, was the year when everyone knew that Tiffany Ambrose was the front-runner. She was a 4.0 student, president of the student council, held the record for the most blood donated by a teenager in Evergreen County, and was beautiful. Everyone hated her. Her only weakness was her talent. What she chose to do was bring her dog onstage and put him through a series of tricks she had taught him. The dog, whose name was Pierre, was a toy poodle—white, trimmed to perfection, and wearing a red kerchief and little black beret. Tiffany put Pierre through his paces; he danced on his hind legs, rolled over, fell over dead when she fired an imaginary shot, and pushed a ball through a small obstacle course. The last of the tricks was a jump through a flaming hoop. Everything went fine until that final trick. Tiffany gave the command, and Pierre started running toward the hoop, sprang perfectly through its center, and bounded off the stage and into the audience. There he began barking and snarling among the panicked spectators. Little girls (who always sat in the front rows) began screaming and running. Parents, who thought their children were at risk from what was surely a rabid French poodle, began running down to the front. In absolute horror, Tiffany raced toward the edge of the stage, but got too close to the hoop and set her dress on fire. She stopped, dropped, and rolled and wasn't hurt, but it only added to the chaos. Of course, there were collisions in the aisle and bumps and bruises and tears, and it took the MC, a very nice but clueless anchor from the local TV station, almost twenty minutes to get everyone settled down again. Later, I found out that the cause of the fiasco was Lauren Lemmlers's brother, Ian, who had strategically placed small piles of beef jerky under the front row of the auditorium seats. Pierre and Tiffany never stood a chance.

I had grown up watching "The Little Miss Christmas Tree" pageant. I sat in the front row as a child and admired all those grown and very beautiful girls, but I knew that it would never be me on that stage.

There were several problems. The first was that I wasn't very ladylike. In fact, I was a tomboy. In spite of my infatuation with the pageant, I would just as soon be out in the woods than out at the mall. Mom was always finding frogs and fungi in my pockets, and I would rather climb a tree than the social ladder. I had two older brothers and my father used to say to them, "You'd better not make Joy mad, because she'll whip you good." I was stronger than both of them. I just never got the girl stuff. Doing nails and hair and makeup just seemed like such a waste of time. I played soccer (although I would have rather played football) and basketball and softball. I wasn't very "girly."

The other problem was related. I wasn't much of a looker. Oh, people didn't run when I came into view. I had pleasant enough features, but I wasn't one of those drop-dead-gorgeous-so-beautiful-that-you-intimidate-boys-so-you-never-have-a-date sort of girls. Ever since I could remember, I wore glasses. Glasses so thick that as a small child I was teased endlessly. That stopped when the other kids knew that I was, as my father would say, "a force to be reckoned with."

So given that I didn't get the girl thing, I was a jock, and I spent most of my life looking through the bottom of pop bottles, I knew it wasn't likely that I would ever make the stage, let alone wear the evergreen crown.

Consequently, my desire to be the winner of Little Miss Christmas Tree was a dream I kept to myself. I knew that if I voiced my desire I would just be laughed at, and besides, it would never happen.

Everyone needs a grandmother. Unfortunately, I didn't have any surviving blood grandparents, but I was lucky enough to be "adopted" by Granny Gunderson. Faith Gunderson lived next door and owned the local hardware store. Although she fit the description of a grandmother agewise, she didn't in the little-old-lady-baking-cookies way. She was also, as my father would say, "a force to be reckoned with." Her husband had died twenty years before and left her the hardware store. She didn't know much about the business, but she learned. Every day, she would tie her long gray hair in a bun, pull a pair of blue overalls over her flannel work shirt, and sell everything from wing nuts to peanuts. Her store was one of those wonderful old wooden floor deals that smells of leather and wax. I spent a lot of time there as a child. I'd stop in after school and watch her make sales, and when I got older, I would help out around the store. It wasn't a very girly thing to do. I could operate a snowblower and forklift by the time I was fourteen. Not the sort of qualities you look for in Little Miss Christmas Tree.

In the summer before my senior year in high school, Granny Gunderson and I were sitting at the counter waiting for customers when she said, "Joy, have you ever thought about the Little Miss Christmas Tree pageant?"

It was the first time anyone had ever asked me that.

"Well, I . . ."

"I just thought that maybe it would be something you'd be interested in."

"I never gave it much thought," I lied.

"Well, you know if you're going to enter you have to have a local business sponsor you and, well, if you wanted to, I'd be glad to do it. I only bring it up now because there's always someone looking for a sponsor, and I wouldn't want to say yes to someone else if you were planning on it."

I was silent for a moment. I had dreamed of the pageant since I was little, but now that I was eligible, the prospect seemed a little overwhelming.

"Well, I'm not sure that it would be such a good idea."

"Why not? You have really good grades, you're very articulate, and you play a mean piano."

I was silent.

"What's wrong?" asked Granny Gunderson. "Don't think you're pretty enough?" She was nothing if she wasn't forthright. "Well, Joy, I'd be lying if I said there weren't prettier girls in town, but real beauty is inside."

Ouch, nothing like being bitten by a cliché.

"You think that's just a cliché," she said, reading my mind. "Well it's true. What really counts is what's inside. And those judges, they think they're looking for the outward beauty, but when someone steps forward with real beauty, the kind that's inside, that's all they see."

I looked at Granny Gunderson, flannel shirt, bibbed overalls, no makeup, and I thought to myself, *I love this woman, but what does she know?*

She looked at me and smiled, and I swear she knew just what I was thinking.

"Fifty years ago," she said.

"Fifty years ago what?" I asked.

"Fifty years ago," she paused, "I was Little Miss Christmas Tree."

"No way!" I exclaimed.

"Way!" she shot back. And she reached under the counter and pulled out an old shoebox. She rummaged around in it for a while and finally produced a yellowed newspaper clipping. "Faith Gunderson Crowned Little Miss Christmas Tree" read the headline. There she was all dolled up in a long gown with the obligatory sash, and on her nose was perched a pair of cat eye glasses. She had all of this blonde hair piled up in a bouffant and another woman was putting the evergreen crown on her.

I stared at the picture and then at Granny and then back at the picture.

"I know a thing or two about this," she said with a twinkle in her eye. "I can make this happen if you want. Go to the Chamber of Commerce and get the paperwork."

I did. And we sat down to fill it out.

We did fine with most of the questions until it came time for "Community Service."

"Well?" said Granny Gunderson.

"Well what?" I replied.

"Don't you have any community service?"

"Well no," I said.

"Joy," she exclaimed, "I'm surprised. Don't you help at the food bank or volunteer for things at church."

"Ah, no," I said, somewhat sheepishly.

"Well, we're going to fix that," she said, and she picked up the phone and dialed a number. "Herbert," she said, "it's Faith Gunderson." They exchanged pleasantries. "Herbert, could you use any volunteers this summer?"

There was some reply from the other end.

"Good!" she said. "I have a young friend who's looking to do some volunteer work and that sounds just right. Tomorrow at noon? Yep, she'll be there. Joy, Joy Thompson. She'll be there at noon." And she hung up.

She looked at me and smiled. "You start tomorrow helping with patients at the Evergreen Nursing Home."

The Evergreen Nursing Home was a large, imposing building that sat on a hill overlooking the town. I had never been and had no interest in ever going there.

"Granny . . ." I began.

"Don't Granny me," she said. "You know, Joy, Little Miss Christmas Tree aside, you should be giving something back."

"Giving something back?"

"Yes," she said. "You've been blessed with great health and a quick mind, and there are others less fortunate."

"But an old people's home?"

"What's wrong with old people?" she challenged.

I was speechless.

"Joy, life is only worth living when you give of yourself. That's the real meaning of Christmas. God sent his son as a gift, we give gifts at Christmas to remember that, but all of life is a gift, and it needs to be given away to others. You should be doing this even if you don't enter the pageant."

The only reason I would ever do something like this is because of the pageant, I thought to myself. But all I could manage was an "Okay."

The next day at noon, I reported to Herbert Dixon's office. Mr. Dixon was a balding middle-aged man whose enthusiasm for his work was unbounded.

"Well you must be Joy Thompson," he boomed when I entered his office.

"Yes, I must be," I replied.

"Well, Joy, it's good to have you with us."

"Thank you," I managed.

He picked up the phone and pushed a button.

"Evelyn, would you ask Shirley to step into my office?"

There was an awkward silence and then a knock at the door. When it opened, in walked Shirley Ricketts.

Oh no, I thought, *not Shirley Ricketts*.

Shirley Ricketts was a classmate, not that I had ever spoken to her. It's funny how even in a small school the classes segregate themselves. I was never in the popular group; I hung out with the jocks. I sure hadn't sunk as low as Shirley's group. Shirley was one of those kids hardly anybody spoke to. She was shy and nerdy and was the kind of girl your mother would say "had a pretty face." That was code for fat. Kids used to say that she was so overweight, it would have been better if she had rickets. Kids can be so cruel.

"Hi, Joy," she said cheerfully, as though we had just talked the day before.

"Hey, Shirley," I managed.

"Shirley," said Mr. Dixon, "Joy is here to volunteer. Why don't you take her to the dining room and see where she can be of help."

And so Shirley Ricketts led me down the hall to the dining room.

"You do this much?" I asked.

"Every day," she said. That pretty much exhausted my conversational abilities.

We entered the dining room, which was large with round tables. At each table sat three or four patients. Some were feeding themselves, but others sat motionless with their plates in front of them.

"Hello, Mrs. Walters," said Shirley enthusiastically. She was addressing a disheveled old woman who was tied to her wheelchair. "Isn't it a grand day?" she said gleefully.

Even though I had been there only a few minutes, I could tell there was no way on God's green earth that Mrs. Walters was going to respond.

"Mrs. Walters, this is Joy Thompson," Shirley said with the same enthusiasm. "She's going to help with your lunch."

I looked at Shirley. "Help with lunch? What does that mean?"

"It's very simple," Shirley said, as if addressing a child. "Just take a spoonful from her tray and put it in her mouth. She'll do the rest. Oh, and another thing," she said, "make sure you talk to her. She really is in there."

I sat down in front of Mrs. Walters. She was looking at the ceiling. There was a bowl of some sort of oatmeal-looking stuff in front of her and another bowl of green Jell-O.

I picked up the spoon, put some oatmeal on it, and placed it in Mrs. Walters's mouth. She took it and began to work it around. Then it all came back out.

"Shirley!" I cried.

Shirley came back over. "It's okay, Joy," she said, "just try it again." And she stood there for the next spoonful, which was more successful, before she moved on.

This is disgusting, I thought, as I continued to shovel food into Mrs. Walters's mouth. *There's got to be something else I can do for my community service. This is positively degrading.*

After Mrs. Walters, I fed Mr. Prentiss and then Mrs. Hartzell, and then I was asked to help one of the nurses. I won't even describe what that entailed; it was just too disgusting for words.

"Joy Thompson, I am absolutely ashamed of you!" said Granny Gunderson.

I had returned from the nursing home to the hardware store complaining mightily and swearing I wasn't going back.

"It's too disgusting?" she said incredulously. "This from a girl who had a fungus collection at the age of eight!"

I was a little embarrassed.

"Joy, you will be going back."

"Why?"

"Because it's the right thing to do. You need to learn that we find meaning in life by serving others—by giving our lives as a gift. And if you can't do that," she intoned, "then you certainly don't deserve to wear the crown."

"I'm not sure it's worth Little Miss Christmas Tree," I said.

"I'm not talking about that," she said. "I'm talking about a heavenly crown. The one you get when God says, 'Well done, good and faithful servant.' That's the only crown that matters."

And so I went back. Not happily, but I went back. And something funny happened. Shirley Ricketts and I became friends. I watched her around the home, and she was nothing but pleasant and happy. She spoke to every patient with love and respect. She did what she was asked, not only without complaining, but with . . .

joy. When I discovered that, I was really embarrassed. If anyone should be expressing "joy," it should be me. And the other funny thing that happened was that Shirley's appearance didn't matter anymore. Actually, I just didn't notice. The fact that she was overweight and not very attractive wasn't even an issue because (and this was a huge revelation) there was something inside her I admired. Something beautiful.

One afternoon, we were taking a break.

"You know, Shirley," I said, "I really admire you."

Shirley didn't respond. She looked at the ground.

"I watch you move among these patients and you're so genuine. You really like these folks, and well, I just wanted you to know that I admire that."

She looked up and a tear fell from her eye.

"What's wrong?" I said. "I didn't mean to . . ."

"No," she said, "it's all right. It's just that no one has ever said that to me before. You know, school is a pretty lonely place. I don't have many friends, and I look at you and others and wish I was," and she paused here for a deep breath, "more like you."

I was stunned. "More like me?" I said.

"Yeah, you know, you're funny and self-confident and nothing ever seems to bother you, and you have a lot of friends."

I was silent for a moment. "Shirley, you hang on to what you have because it's better than anything I have. You really know how to love these people." And then I told her the truth, that the only reason I was doing this was for the Little Miss Christmas Tree pageant.

She smiled through another tear and said, "I know."

I started to laugh and so did she and from then on we were friends.

I told this to Granny, and she smiled. "It's about time you caught on," she said. "The beauty that counts is inside, and the crown that counts is eternal." But then she said, "We're going to the mall."

She closed up the shop, we got in her truck, and drove the forty miles to Evergreen Mall.

"What are we doing?" I asked.

"Well, it is true that it's the inner beauty that's most important, but it doesn't hurt to polish the outside a bit."

We spent the afternoon working on the outward thing. The first stop was to the optometrist. Granny had made an appointment for me with Dr. Stuart, who gave me the once-over and said to her, "Yeah, we can do that."

"Do what?" I asked.

"Contacts," said Granny.

Then we went to the fancy department store and took a seat at the cosmetics counter. I wasn't all that thrilled with this, but we spent over an hour with a "consultant," who gave me all kinds of advice and "made me up."

"Wow," said Granny when I was done.

I looked in the mirror. "I can't go to school looking like this," I said.

"And why not?"

"Because I have a reputation to defend," I said. "I can't intimidate an opposing player on the soccer field looking like this!"

Granny laughed.

"Well how about we buy what we need, write down the secret formula, and save it for the pageant?" she said. And that's what we did, and then we picked up my contacts.

School started in September, and I would see Shirley in the halls. We talked and laughed, but we didn't really hang together. Still it was good to see her, and I considered her to be a friend.

In October, I was sitting at the lunch table, and Alice Martinet came over and sat down. Alice was one of the most popular girls in school, blonde hair (not her real color), blue eyes, and way too much time on the tanning bed.

"You'll never believe this," she said.

I didn't like Alice. She was one of those girls whom the teachers all thought was sweetness and light, but once you got to know her, you realized she flew to school every day on a broom.

"What?" I said.

"Guess who's entered the pageant?" she said, relishing the moment.

"Who?" I asked.

"Ricketts," she laughed. "Can you imagine? I thought it was funny enough when you entered but Ricketts? She must be nuts."

"Alice," I said.

"Yeah?"

"I think you'd better go, your flying monkeys are calling." And I got up and left.

That afternoon I told Granny.

"So?" she said.

"Well, I don't know. It's just that, well, I'm worried she'll embarrass herself."

"Embarrass herself?"

"Granny, she's an overweight nerd."

"I beg your pardon."

"I mean, she's not really pageant material."

Granny's eyes narrowed at me, and then I got it.

"Yeah, yeah, I know, neither am I, but . . ."

"But nothing," said Granny. "You shouldn't care what the world thinks. You need to be her friend."

"I am her friend."

"Then start acting like it. You're the one who told me you admire her. You see something there that others don't; maybe the judges will too. Don't you think she knows what she's doing? You'd better love her. She'll need that now."

The next day in school I found Shirley in the cafeteria and sat down.

"Hey," she said.

"Hey, yourself," I replied. "Heard you're in the pageant. Who's your sponsor?"

"Edelstein's," she replied.

This was going from bad to worse. Edelstein's was the local chocolate shop.

She looked at me, but didn't say anything immediately.

"I'm the laughingstock of the school," she said.

"Well let 'em laugh," I said. "They're laughing at me too."

"Not as much as at me," said Shirley.

"Hey, this isn't a contest," I said.

"Yes, it is," said Shirley, and then we both started to laugh.

"I admire you," I said.

"Thanks, I appreciate it." And then she said, "I need a favor."

"Yeah?"

"I'm going to sing for my talent, and I need an accompanist. I know it's a lot to ask because your competing too but . . ."

I didn't even let her finish. "Bring me the music and tell me when you want to start rehearsing."

I had never heard Shirley sing before. She chose an aria by Mozart, which was difficult, but she was good. I mean really good.

One day Alice stopped me in the hall. "I guess Shirley will have to go last at the pageant," she said.

I wasn't going to bite but she went on.

"Because, you know, it's all over when the fat lady sings." And she waltzed off. Oh, I hated that girl.

The weeks flew by and Christmas drew near. The day of the pageant finally arrived. We put Granny's plan into action, and I did the makeup just like I was taught and wore my contacts (for the first time). When I arrived at school that afternoon for the interview the first person I ran into was Alice Martinet.

"Good grief, Thompson," she said. "You look like the Avon lady exploded."

That did it. I had had enough of that girl. Her self-righteous, sanctimonious, better-than-everyone-else tone—the way she belittled everybody. I snapped. I clenched my fist and reared back with every intention of breaking her cute little upturned nose. Alice's eyes widened as she realized she had gone one step too far, and then I heard:

"Hey, Alice! Hey, Joy! Wow, Joy, don't you look great." I turned around, fist still clenched, to see Shirley.

I had never noticed how beautiful she really was until that moment. Someone had helped her, but she wasn't overdone. She just looked, well, beautiful.

"Shirley," I said, "you look terrific." and when we turned, Alice was gone. "Thanks," I said.

That evening, we returned for the program. All of the girls gathered in the cafeteria and waited for their turn to go onstage. First, we all went out individually, walked across the stage, and paused at several different places (this was the "poise" portion of the contest). This was done alphabetically. I'm not sure, but I could have sworn that when I stepped out onstage there was a little gasp of surprise. However, when Shirley went out there was laughter. Not loud, boisterous laughter, but the little tittering of small-minded, small-town idiots. When she came offstage I was waiting for her.

"You okay?"

"Yeah."

"You wouldn't lie to me, would you?"

"Maybe this was a mistake."

"Shirley," I said, "look at me." And she did. "You're better than they are, and we're going to show them. Right?"

"Right," she said, but without a lot of enthusiasm.

When that was over, we did the talent. The order was chosen at random, and I was on early. Shirley was on a couple of acts after I was. I played my piece just fine, as well as I ever had, and went back to the cafeteria to wait to go on with Shirley.

When I got there a small group of girls was huddled in the corner laughing. It was obvious that Alice was up to something.

"What's going on?" I asked.

"Nothing, Thompson," snickered Alice, and she wandered off.

Several minutes later, I heard a scream from the same corner of the room. Turning around, I could see Shirley. She was jumping around as white as could be and screaming. I ran over to her.

"Shirley, what's wrong?"

"My-my bag," she stuttered. "My-my bag."

"What about your bag?"

"My bag," she said again.

The bag where she had her stuff, including her music, was sitting on the floor. I leaned down and opened it. A little white mouse ran out. Shirley screamed again.

"Ricketts, you're on in three," called a voice from the hallway.

Over in the other corner Alice and a group of girls were laughing.

"Shirley," I said, "are you okay?"

She nodded, but I knew she wasn't.

"Ricketts, you're on in two," said the voice.

"Shirley, we have to go on. Pull yourself together." I took her hand and pulled her down the hallway and into the wings of the auditorium stage.

The MC announced her name and we walked out. Shirley was still pale. I sat down at the piano. Shirley stared blankly at the audience. I played the first several bars of Mozart and . . . nothing. I stopped, as if I were confused, and started again . . . nothing.

I have no idea what possessed me, but I stood up from the piano bench and walked the short distance to where Shirley was standing. The audience was murmuring. I turned my back to them.

"Shirley," I said, "you can do this. No, you *will* do this. You will not let us down. You've come too far, taken too many risks. You're beautiful. I think you can win this." Shirley looked at me. And then I said, "You know I love you, right?"

A small tear appeared in her eye, and she nodded and said, "I'm ready."

I turned to the audience and said, "Please, excuse me. It's my fault; I was confused." I sat down and played, and Shirley sang, but it wasn't what she was capable of. It wasn't bad, but it didn't soar like in rehearsal. She had made an amazing recovery, but it wasn't complete.

When this is all over I will *break Alice Martinet's nose!* I thought.

The rest of the evening was a blur, and the next thing I knew, all twenty of us were standing onstage, waiting for the announcement of the winners. There was a tradition that the girls all held hands when this was done, and I purposely left my place in line and stood next to Shirley to hold her hand.

"Thanks," she said. "I love you too."

I know we're not going to win, but if there is a God in heaven, neither will Alice, I thought to myself.

"The second runner-up for Little Miss Christmas Tree and the winner of a $1,000 college scholarship is . . . Ashley Johnson." That was good news. Ashley had done well; she deserved it.

"The first runner-up for Little Miss Christmas Tree, and the winner of a $2,500 college scholarship is . . . Shirley Ricketts."

The entire world went into slow motion. I can still remember turning toward Shirley, who looked like someone had just shot her, and then she broke into the biggest, most beautiful smile I had ever seen and put her arms around me so tight I thought she was going to break every bone in my body. She left the line and received her check and sash. I could not have been happier.

"And now the moment you've all been waiting for," said the MC.

"Anyone but Alice, anyone but Alice," I kept saying.

"This year's Little Miss Christmas Tree is . . . Joy Thompson."

It was at this exact moment that the entire world stood still. I was so intent on not hearing Alice's name that I didn't hear mine. Then, when things did start to move again, I couldn't hear anything, and then it all came in a tremendous roar. The other girls hugging me and pushing me forward, flashbulbs going off, and a big sash laid across my shoulder, and then there was Granny.

"Presenting the crown to our winner is Faith Gunderson, Joy's sponsor and the winner of Little Miss Christmas Tree fifty years ago." The auditorium burst into applause again. Granny placed the crown on my head.

"I'm proud of you," she said.

Then I heard the audience say "oh" and, turning around, saw that Alice Martinet had fainted and was lying on the stage in a most unladylike repose. "There is a God after all!" I said to Granny.

We lingered in the auditorium for a long time. My parents were just as pleased as could be. And Granny said again, "I'm proud of you."

"Thanks," I said.

"Know why? It's not because you won."

"No?"

"It's because of what you did for Shirley."

"You're the one who taught me to be a friend."

"Well, you done good tonight," said Granny.

I basked in the glory of the moment. Here was the thing I'd dreamed about since I was a little girl, and I finally got it. Against all odds and in spite of everyone's expectations, I had finally realized my dream.

I went back to the cafeteria to get my things. As I walked down the hallway, I passed several of the judges. They were standing in a corner talking. And I heard one of them say, "Too bad about the Ricketts girl. If she had nailed the talent she would have won."

My heart, which had moments ago been higher than I could have ever imagined, sank to an unspeakable depth. Suddenly, I realized that I was the beneficiary of Alice Martinet's dirty trick.

I didn't sleep much that night, and the next day, I lay in my bed most of the day and looked at the sash and the evergreen crown. I had no joy. I thought about what Granny had told me about Christmas. That it was about giving, about a God who gave his son for us and how we give to remind each other of that great gift. But most importantly, that if we don't give ourselves, our lives might just be wasted. I thought about Shirley. Shirley who did community service because she wanted to, and who really loved those old people, and how she had taken such an enormous risk in the pageant, and how she had taught me that beauty really does come from the inside out. She was the most beautiful person I ever met.

It was almost dinnertime when I told my parents. They said they were proud of me and asked me if I wanted a ride. I said no. I was going to stop at Granny's first and then walk. I went next door and told her, too. She gave me a huge hug and told me how much she loved me and how proud she was of me. But I was only doing what was right.

I headed off down the street in the snow. It was Christmas Eve. The evening we remember the great gift of Jesus. There were carolers somewhere in the distance. "Glory to the newborn King," they sang. I squeezed the crown in my hand.

The doorbell rang, and Shirley stood there looking at me.

"Hey," I said.

"Hey, yourself."

There was an awkward silence and then, "This belongs to you," I said, holding out the evergreen crown.

"Oh no, Joy. Please don't."

"No," I said. "If it hadn't been for Alice you would have won, and I would have been runner-up. I can't be Little Miss Christmas Tree. It wouldn't be right."

We both started to cry.

"Well," she said, "only if we split the scholarship even."

I started to laugh. "Deal," I said.

And that was the best Christmas I ever had. It was the best because I got to give away the thing that was most important to me. And got to give it to someone I really loved. My gift that Christmas, the gift that was given to me, was that I was able to give it all away. I was able to give away the thing I had hoped for since I was a little girl, and I did it with joy. It was like what God had done for me that first Christmas. Given me his son, the most important thing to him, and he did it for love.

5

THE THREE WISE GUYS

I'm driving north on a beautiful December afternoon with my two sons sitting next to me and a Christmas tree in the bed of my pickup.

Christmas isn't really Christmas without a Christmas tree. Oh, I know you can have Christmas under any circumstances, even cast away on a desert island with only sand and coconut palms, but to *really* have Christmas you've got to have a tree. A live tree. An evergreen. Granted, there are some pretty amazing artificial trees out there, the kind that you get right up to with the watering can before you realize that someone had taken it out of a box the week before. But that's not really a Christmas tree.

A real Christmas tree has to be cut down and brought in out of the snow, dragged across the front hall and into the living room, where cold air escapes from deep within its branches and begins to fill the room with the rich aroma of pine. It stands there bare and unadorned until the family gathers to string on the lights (I'm partial to the little white ones myself) and hang the ornaments, each carrying its own memory of a Christmas past. Baby's first Christmas, the colored paper ornament made in nursery school, the ceramic ones made in high school art class, the ugly one you never would have bought but you display anyway because it was given to you by your parents the first year you were married. The finale, the crowning touch, a beautiful angel, tops it all off. There's nothing like sitting in the room with only the tree lights on and maybe a fire in the fireplace on a cold winter's night.

For my father there was one other requirement for a Christmas tree: you had to cut it yourself. Every year we'd drive out to the Happy Star Tree Farm with a hand saw and tramp around in the snow until we found the perfect tree. The larger the family got, the more difficult this became, because everyone had an opinion. "No, there's a bare spot on this side." "Nope, too thin at the top." "This one's too bushy at the bottom." Thus, we'd wander around in the snow until dusk, when we'd finally agree on the perfect tree.

Then we'd drag it up the hill to the car and Dad would tie it on the top, accompanied by Mom's mantra, "Make sure it's tight enough," while the baby would be eating snow and I would be putting the same down the back of my sister's snowsuit. Then we'd all pile back into the car and take our prize home. Not only was it an important ritual, but it seemed to generate some of the family's favorite stories. Like the year Dad lowered the windows and tied the tree to the roof through them, with the unintended consequence of tying all the doors shut, prompting him to make all of us, including Mom, climb through the windows to get into the car. Or the year it was so cold—and at this point everyone sitting around the dinner table, hearing the story for the umpteenth time, would say, "How cold was it?" and Dad would retort, "We got out of the car and cut the first one we came to and got the heck out of there." Mom would add that it took her longer to get our galoshes on us than it did to select the tree that year.

That's the way getting Christmas trees used to be in my family, until I was twelve, that is, because nothing would ever top the story of the tree we cut when I was eleven and Carol was nine, Robby was six, and Sara, the baby, was four. It started out as usual: We all piled into the Plymouth Suburban station wagon, the baby in front between Mom and Dad, and the rest of us in back poking and taunting each other the way kids do.

It was a typically cold December day, but we took our time seeking the perfect tree. After a couple of hours considering all sorts of evergreens, we found one to our liking, cut it down, dragged it to the car, tied it to the top, and drove it home. Dad declared the hunt "seamless."

He got out the tree stand, cut the bottom off the tree, tightened the stand around it, and carried the tree into the house. It was a magnificent specimen, barely fitting the nine-foot height of the living room. We all stood in admiration and Mom proclaimed, as always, "I think this is the best tree we've ever had!"

Dad reached into the decoration trunk to get the first strand of lights when we heard something unusual, a rustling sound, coming from the tree. As if by instinct, we all froze in place and listened. Then it came again—a quick rustling, as though something was adjusting itself deep within the branches. And then it jumped. Or rather, I should say, *they* jumped.

I had never seen a flying squirrel before, let alone two. Out from the branches they leapt, then, to the accompaniment of our impromptu chorus of gasps, darted across the floor in due haste, making a fast break for the front window, which, of course, was closed. They banged against the glass and fell back, momentarily stunned, then darted up the drapes and perched, frozen, on the drapery rod.

The whole family was stunned, but the dogs knew what to do. Our two golden retrievers, beloved eighty-five-pound Beauregard, on his last legs, and Spooner, just a year old, both sprang into action as if their family was being attacked by pork chops. They charged at the window, Spooner smacking against the glass, but Beauregard, being slower, galloped directly at the drapery. As he tugged fabric and rod to the floor, the squirrels soared (you cannot imagine how far a flying squirrel can jump—maybe twenty feet!) to the mantel, where they knocked over several unlit candles in crystal candlesticks, then sprang to the window at the opposite side of the room and into more drapery. By now the whole family was fully involved in the drama. Mom screamed, the baby cried, Dad muttered miscellaneous exclamations. Carol and Robby banged heads trying to flee the scene and crashed into heap on the floor. The dogs changed directions and charged to the opposite side of the room after the squirrels, but the squirrels took off again in different directions, one to the side of the room and under the couch, with Spooner in pursuit, and the other back across the length of the room and into the safety of the tree. Beauregard lunged, knocking the tree over on top of Carol and Robby.

Amid the chaos, we watched helplessly as the squirrels exited the room and disappeared into the house. No one was hurt, but my mother was absolutely hysterical, insisting that we all vacate the house except for Dad, apparently now considered to be the great white hunter, whom she charged with ridding the house of, as she termed it, "those vermin." This was easier said than done, of course, and we actually had to check into a nearby hotel for two nights until my father was able to trap the stowaways in a Havahart trap and release them several miles from the house. To us kids, this became known as the "Vermin Christmas," but to Mom it was always just "*That* Christmas."

The real tragedy was not that the drapes had to be replaced or that to this day Sara gets dizzy when she sees small woodland creatures. No, the real tragedy was that we never had a real Christmas tree again.

"Absolutely not," my mother would intone each year when the topic came up. "I am not going to allow another tree to bring such devastation to my home." It was if there had been two rhinoceros careening around the house instead of a couple of eight-ounce rodents. But she was adamant, and not even my father could dissuade her.

The first year after the incident, when December arrived, Mom announced that she would see to the tree, and several days later we came home from school to find a four-foot aluminum Christmas tree standing in the corner of the living room, illuminated by a spotlight with a round multicolored lens rotating in front of it so that the tree changed from blue to green to red with each rotation.

"I'll bet if we hook it up to the TV we can get Channel Six," my father offered unhelpfully.

For the rest of my time at home, that was our Christmas tree. I couldn't stand it. I made up my mind that when the time came and I was out on my own, I would never, ever, ever have an artificial tree. My tree would have to be real, and fresh cut, and I wouldn't care if it came with grizzly bears in it.

But that's not the reason I'm driving north now with a Christmas tree in my truck. I'm doing this because . . . well, because I got arrested while I was in college. Yes. I'm sad to admit that truth, but in some ways it was the best thing that ever happened to me.

McKinley College is a private school of a couple thousand students about three hours north of where I grew up. It's the kind of school where everybody is terribly earnest about changing the world and students gather into the wee hours discussing weighty matters that really aren't. When you say you graduated from McKinley, everyone says, "Oh, that's a good school."

My junior year I lived in a house the school owned. Groups of students with a common interest could cast their lot together and apply for off-campus housing in one of the big old Victorian homes the school had snatched up twenty-odd years earlier. Six of us had gone together and applied for residency in one of these houses because we were Christians. Three seniors lived in the bedrooms at the back of the house, and my two closest friends, Clarence, who, for reasons known only to his family, was always called Buddy, and Marcus and I lived in a massive room in the front. The first floor, with its kitchen, living, and dining room, was common space. We three juniors had all been on the same floor freshman year and had become good friends.

The whole street comprised these "special interest" houses except for one. There was one elderly lady who wouldn't sell to the school. Mrs. Tannenbaum lived alone next door to us and she was a mean old cuss. She never had anything nice to say to anyone. She complained constantly to the police about every slight, real and imagined. Music was too loud, someone walked on her grass, there was trash in her yard, any miscellaneous gripe, and she always blamed us.

This really angered me, and I spent a lot of time thinking about getting even. When she complained that there was a paper cup on her front lawn and naturally blamed us, I told the guys I was thinking about emptying a Dumpster on her front lawn.

"Tom, what's the matter with you?" asked Buddy. "You're supposed to be a Christian."

"And I am," I said.

"Well start acting like it. Don't do mean things to people. Don't even think about it."

"Tell me this doesn't bother you."

"Of course it does, but I'm not going to sink to her level. What we need to do is be genuinely kind to the lady."

"Be kind to her?!" I said incredulously. "She doesn't deserve 'kind.'"

"No, she doesn't, but neither do we."

"What are you talking about?"

"Don't flatter yourself, Tom. You think that as long as there's somebody more difficult than you, then you're okay. Well, you're not. You've got to love people, despite their faults. If it's deserved, it isn't love."

"Huh?"

"Tom, love is given freely. It's grace. Not because you deserve it, but because someone chose to love you."

"Who?"

"God."

"And . . . ?"

". . . and so you're supposed to, actually, you're *empowered* to love others." And then he added, "Even Mrs. Tannenbaum."

So Buddy and Marcus commenced "Operation Grace."

"Good morning, Mrs. Tannenbaum," Marcus would say.

"Stupid boy," she would say. "Mind your own business."

"Beautiful day, isn't it, Mrs. Tannenbaum?"

No response.

Later that autumn they took it upon themselves to rake her leaves. She never acknowledged it.

Still they persisted. They would win her over. They would be kinder than she was cantankerous.

I just didn't understand. Why be nice to such a curmudgeon? But I figured if that's what Buddy and Marcus wanted to do, they could have at it.

And then one day the ice began to melt. It was early December and it had snowed about six inches overnight. The school required us to keep the walks clean, and it was my turn at the task, so I went out with the shovel. As I finished, I noticed that all of the other walks were shoveled except for the one next door. Mrs. Tannenbaum's. *Oh, what the heck,* I thought, and I shoveled the public sidewalk and the walk down to the curb, and then, without thinking, continued with the walk up to the front porch, up the porch stairs, and was cleaning off the snow that had blown up onto the porch when I heard the door open. My back was to it and I was scared to turn around. I had never been this close to the cause of so much unpleasantness. But then I heard a voice say, "Thank you."

I turned to see Mrs. Tannenbaum stepping out onto the porch. I instinctively took off my knit cap. "You're welcome, ma'am," I said.

"You boys, you're different."

"We get that a lot," I said, making an attempt at humor.

"No, really," she said. "Every other year the kids in that house are real trouble."

"I'm sorry to hear that," I said.

"Well," she said, somewhat awkwardly, "I just wanted to say thank you."

I stuck out my hand. "Tom Montgomery," I offered.

"Nice to meet you, Tom Montgomery," she said, taking my hand.

I put on my cap and started down the steps. God only knows, and I mean that literally, only God knows why I did this, but I turned back and said, "Did you get your Christmas tree yet?"

"I don't get Christmas trees," she said, and her sadness was tangible. She slipped back inside before I could say anything else.

"Mrs. Tannenbaum doesn't get a Christmas tree?" Buddy repeated incredulously when I relayed my little conversation with the neighbor to Marcus and him that afternoon. "That's ironic!"

"Why?" asked Marcus, genuinely not getting it.

"Marcus," I said, "*Tannenbaum—Christmas tree.* Mrs. *Tannenbaum* doesn't get a *Christmas* tree."

"Oh, I see," he said, but it was plain that he didn't. Marcus has an IQ of 170 but doesn't get knock-knock jokes. "Maybe she's Jewish."

"No! And besides, she was wearing a cross on a chain around her neck," I said.

"Maybe she wears a cross because she's Swiss," Buddy offered humorously. Now Marcus was really confused.

I shook my head. "She's a widow. I'll bet she can't afford a tree."

"Well, let's get her one," exclaimed Buddy.

"Yeah," said Marcus. "Let's buy one and leave it on her front porch."

"Wait," I said. "That's no good. She'd never get it in the house by herself."

"Well, we can't very well waltz into her house uninvited and set the thing up," said Buddy.

And then I said the words that would seal our fate. "Why not?"

The more we thought about it, the more we liked the idea. We'd get the tree and take it to her house at night when she was asleep, set it up, and leave. She'd never know how it got there, and she wouldn't have to go without a Christmas tree. What a great surprise this would be, as though Santa had really paid her a visit. It would be a kind, yes, even a loving, thing to do.

Unfortunately, there were a few kinks to be worked out, not the least of which was money. Pooling all of our resources, we came up with twelve dollars and fifteen cents, including the Canadian quarter Marcus found under a couch cushion. That would probably be enough for the stand but not for the tree.

"We could cut our own," offered Buddy.

"We'd still have to pay for it," I said.

"Not if we went up into the woods," he replied.

So we piled in Marcus's old Buick and drove into town, where we found a stand for eleven dollars.

Later that night we drove out to the woods behind the athletic fields to look for a tree. This was a mistake, of course, as it occurred to me that we should have found one when it was light out, cut it down, and stashed it somewhere. But here we were in snow a foot deep, with flashlights on a moonless night in the middle of the woods.

"Over here!" yelled Marcus.

He had found a seven-foot pine tree that didn't look all that bad. I had never before realized that wild trees lack the same symmetry of farmed trees, which are trimmed and pruned. It was five degrees below zero with the wind chill factor, so we decided that this specimen would do. Using a camp saw we'd borrowed from some friends in the environmental sciences department, we cut it down, dragged it out of the woods, across the baseball field, and over to Marcus's Buick.

"Now what?" asked Marcus.

"Now we tie it to the top and take it home."

"Tie it with what?"

"You didn't bring any rope?"

"Where was I going to get rope?" protested Marcus.

And so we lifted the tree onto the roof, and Buddy and I rolled down the back windows and sat on the doors with our legs inside and the rest of us outside holding the tree on the roof while Marcus cautiously drove us back.

Now I was really cold.

We pulled into the alley behind our house and Buddy went in to get the stand. I reached into the tree and started to feel around.

"What are you doing?" asked Marcus.

"Checking for squirrels," I said.

"What?"

"I'll tell you later."

We put the stand on the tree and stood in our backyard looking at each other.

"Are we really going to do this?" asked Marcus.

"Absolutely," I said.

We carried the tree quietly into Mrs. Tannenbaum's yard and up onto the back porch. Then it suddenly occurred to us we didn't have a plan for getting into the house.

"Great," said Buddy. "Now what do we do?"

Marcus turned to retreat down the steps, but slipped on the ice, and, flailing wildly in an attempt to regain his balance, knocked an empty planter off the porch. He landed faceup in the snow, arms and legs spread like he was about to make a snow angel. I suppressed the urge to laugh at the sight.

"I'm okay," he whispered.

"I don't believe it!" I said.

"Sorry," began Marcus.

"No," I said. "Look!"

And lying on the porch, where the planter had been, was a key.

Marcus got up and brushed himself off. At the sight of the key, his jaw dropped. "Must be a sign from God," he said.

I put the key in the back door lock. Before turning it, I instructed, "Now, we must be absolutely silent. Buddy, you go in first and clear a way, and Marcus and I will carry the tree in behind you."

It's not easy carrying a sizeable Christmas tree into a house. It's even harder to do it in the dark, in an unfamiliar house, in utter silence.

Marcus had the top of the tree and I had the trunk, following Buddy, who moved some kitchen chairs to create a path. Even in the darkness I could see Buddy's form clearly. He was taking exaggerated steps and had his arms stretched out above his head and his wrists cocked, looking like some strange bird.

"Buddy," I hissed, "what are you doing?"

Buddy turned, approaching me in the same strange posture, and when his face was inches from mine, whispered, "Christmas ninja."

I started to laugh, then checked myself, but the more I tried to stop, the funnier the whole thing got, and short little bursts of laughter began to pop from my mouth.

"Shhh," said Buddy, and slapped my cheek. Crack!

We all froze in place. Tears streamed down my face, either from the suppressed laughter or the slap, I couldn't tell. We stood motionless for what seemed like an eternity, until finally Buddy turned and continued into the house.

We found the living room without difficulty and quickly determined not to move any furniture. We set the tree up in the middle of the room. It really filled the space. Christmas trees always look smaller outdoors than inside.

We stood in the dark, silently admiring our work, and then Buddy whispered, "I think it's the best tree we've ever had."

I started to laugh again, but an unfamiliar man's voice came from the darkness behind us.

"Don't move. Put your hands where I can see them." A huge beam of flashlight blinded us.

The room light flipped on and there stood two policemen with drawn guns pointed at us. No one was laughing now.

They actually handcuffed us and took us downtown in the police cruiser.

The station didn't have a jail cell big enough for three people, so we were escorted to a small conference room. It had a table, four chairs, a coffeepot, and insulated paper cups on a stand. Decorating the walls in big frames were uniform patches from other police departments around the world.

One of the officers came in after a while and sat down.

"Want to tell me what you were doing?"

And so we did. We told him about Mrs. Tannenbaum and how she had been so cranky, but then she was sort of being nice, and how she didn't have a tree, and how we thought we'd surprise her with one.

He was writing all this down.

"Where'd you get the tree?"

"From the woods behind the college's athletic fields."

He wrote that down, too, and got up to leave the room.

"Excuse me, but may I ask where you're going, officer?" asked Marcus.

"In this county, we deal with this sort of stuff when it happens," he said. "The magistrate is coming in to see you boys."

That did not sound good.

And so, at nearly four in the morning, the three of us found ourselves seated in a small courtroom in the same building as the police offices, staring at our shoes and trying not to make eye contact with Judge Hartman.

Judge Hartman was big and silver-haired, a thoroughly imposing presence in his judicial robes, and looked as though he might be inclined to recommend the death penalty for us. He sat at his judicial desk on the dais, flanked by witness chairs to his left and right, sifting through some papers.

"Well . . ." he sighed, drawing out the word, shaking his head almost imperceptibly, addressing no one in particular as he reviewed the last of the papers. "Now I think I've seen it all." After a seemingly interminable silence, he looked at us over his reading glasses.

"Will the three wise guys please rise," he intoned.

We bounced to our feet.

"Boys, you know you're guilty of breaking and entering."

We all said, "Ah, yes, sir," though we'd never entertained the possibility that our deed could be considered a crime, and this was the first we'd heard a charge.

"What is wrong with you three?" he asked. "You just can't go into people's houses and set up Christmas trees. It's just not done."

"Yes, sir," we all chimed. "We're very sorry, sir," Marcus added.

"Well, you should be. You nearly frightened poor old Mrs. Tannenbaum to death, and you could have been shot."

"Yes, sir," we responded in unison, although that possibility hadn't occurred to us either. This was just awful. My stomach was in knots.

"However, Mrs. Tannenbaum doesn't want to press charges."

Suddenly there was a ray of hope.

"Does that mean we can go?" asked Marcus.

"No, it does *not* mean you can go," stated the judge. "There's still the issue of destruction of public property."

"Destruction of public property?"

"The tree, boys, the tree. That tree you cut was on town property. You just can't go anywhere you like and cut down trees."

Another thought that hadn't occurred to us.

"Fifty dollars," he pronounced firmly, then slammed the wooden gavel on his desk.

"Fifty dollars?" repeated Buddy, stunned.

"Don't you boys have fifty dollars?"

"If we had fifty dollars, we'd have bought a tree!" blurted Buddy, flirting with a tone that had great potential to get us yet deeper into trouble.

I'm not certain, but the judge may have suppressed a smile.

"The fine has to be paid, boys, and it must be paid before you can leave."

We looked at each other blankly. What were we to do? It was 4 a.m. and none of us had family nearby. My parents, 150 miles away, were the nearest, and they would be none too happy to receive a phone call from me now.

Then Judge Hartman did a most extraordinary thing. He rose from his desk, removed his robe, stepped down from the dais, and walked over to us. He reached into his back pocket, pulled out his wallet, removed two twenties and a ten, and handed the bills to Buddy.

"Here you go, boys," he said. "I'll pay the price for you. Merry Christmas."

"Thank you, sir," we said in stunned disbelief, and looked at each other, our mouths agape.

"One more thing, you three wise guys."

We turned our attention back to the judge. "Yes, sir?"

"Tomorrow you go apologize to Mrs. Tannenbaum and remove the tree from her house."

"Yes, sir." We nodded.

As the police drove us home, I thought about everything that had happened, starting with an old lady who had been so unfair to us, and how Buddy had said we should be nice and extend grace to her anyway. I considered how I myself fell short in so many ways, including this fiasco, yet people still loved me . . . and God still loved me. And I marveled at a wise and compassionate judge who pronounced a fair judgment against us, then paid the price we couldn't pay for our folly. I looked over at Marcus.

"Kind of like what Jesus did for us," he said, as though he'd been reading my thoughts. The truth of Christmas opened up for me right then.

We decided we'd get the pain over with as soon as possible, and so at nine o'clock that morning, the three remorseful wise guys stood in the cold on Mrs. Tannenbaum's porch.

"Well, someone had better get brave and ring the bell," I said.

Marcus reached out and pushed the button. After what seemed like an eternity, the door opened. The three of us stood looking at our shoes, with our hats in our hands.

"Mrs. Tannenbaum . . ." I began.

"Tom Montgomery," she intoned with an indecipherable magnitude. She stepped out into the cold, then threw her arms around me and gave me a great hearty hug, and moved on to Buddy and Marcus.

"Would you all please come in?" she asked.

And we did. Mrs. Tannenbaum led us into the living room, where the tree stood. Now it was covered with lights and ornaments, and underneath it were the parts to an unassembled electric train.

"I think it's the best tree I've ever had," she said, gazing at the tree as though it were a window to another time. "My husband died without warning seven years ago and I took that very hard.

When someone you love dies and leaves you alone, it's very difficult. But nothing has been more difficult than Christmas. We
couldn't have children, you see, and there's no family nearby, and,
why, the thought of trying to get a tree and then decorating it all
by myself without him was just too painful, and so I gave up on
Christmas. But then you three came along. You were kind to me in
spite of my misery, and then you did this!" She gestured at the
tree.

"Well, uh, we're really. . ."

But she interrupted, "It's the nicest thing anybody's done for
me in years. You boys have given me back Christmas." And she
swept us up in her arms again like we were her lost sons.

And that's what we became—her adopted sons. The next year
we actually lived with her and took care of the lawn and the leaves
and the snow, and fell in love with this precious old lady. We
shared stories and laughter and amazing dinners with her. That
December we took Mrs. Tannenbaum out to cut a tree, legally,
and strung the little white lights and helped decorate, as Buddy
termed it, Mrs. Tannenbaum's tannenbaum.

In "giving back Christmas" to Mrs. Tannenbaum, to borrow her
phrase, I also came to grasp the meaning of Christmas in a deeper
way. I realized that, at its core, Christmas isn't about trees and
decorations, and that it is about something much deeper than just
being kind. It is about a God who sees fit to pay the price for our
folly. Christmas is about God bringing his grace into the world in
the form of Jesus because we need it, not because we could ever
do anything to deserve or earn it.

And so every December I make this trip north. I pull the truck
up to the curb, and my sons jump out into the snowbank. I hoist
the tree from the bed, up the sidewalk, and onto the porch. The
three of us stand there while I ring the bell. A very special old lady
opens the door, steps out into the cold, and gives me a great big
bear hug.

"Hello, Tom Montgomery," she says. "Welcome home."

6

PERSONAL CARE PAGEANT

Until recently, I would have said that I didn't believe in miracles. I do now. It's funny how your life can change in a single moment and when you least expect it. One minute, you're going along with hardly a care, and the next thing you know, everything's different. This is a story about that. Actually it's about two moments. It's tempting to say that the first one was bad and second one good, but if it hadn't been for the first, I never would have experienced the second, the miracle.

My husband and I had moved to Evergreen several months before the accident. Evergreen is a small rural town whose economy is driven by Christmas tree farms. There are twelve in the area, and they support everything we do. The town itself is quite picturesque, and in its center is the "square," which is really a circle with a gazebo in the middle of it. In the summer, on Sunday evenings, bands come and play in the gazebo, and families come to listen. Children dance on the grass. It's really very Norman Rockwellian.

Traffic flows one way around the square—counterclockwise—and consequently, when one is driving, one has a tendency to look left, and when the traffic clears, to pull out from the stop sign. It was a beautiful summer day, bright blue sky; the sun was hot, one of those days that lends itself to daydreaming. I had pulled up to the stop sign and looked left and when the traffic cleared pulled into the intersection. I heard something bang the front of the car. I looked right, and saw nothing, but I put the car in park, got out, and, to my horror, discovered that I had hit a pedestrian. She had come from the proverbial "nowhere." She lay there unconscious, a girl of about eighteen. I had seen her in town before, but didn't know her name.

I called for an ambulance and, of course, the police showed up and took my statement. I was practically hysterical.

The girl's name was Carly Munroe, and she spent the next four weeks in the hospital. Broken pelvis, two broken legs, it would be a long recovery. I almost wished that charges had been filed, but it was ruled an accident. Several witnesses said that she had run out into the crosswalk without stopping. It turned out she was trying to catch a friend. But this sort of event haunts you. I lost my appetite, couldn't sleep for weeks. I was a mess. Of course, in a small town, it was the topic of conversation for everyone. Just when I thought it couldn't get any worse, the newspaper dropped the next bomb: "Local Teen Struck by Car" read the headline, but then the text explained that Carly Munroe was a promising dancer who had a scholarship to an elite arts school in New York where she was going to study ballet. The doctors were worried that she might never walk again, let alone dance.

"Helen, you need to talk to someone," said my husband one evening.

"I do?"

"Sweetheart, you're a mess. You need to move past the accident."

I started to cry. "You just don't understand," I said.

"I know," he said, "I'll never understand it like you do, but I do know that if you don't get some help you're going to be in even deeper trouble. Why don't you go see Father Tom?"

Tom McNabb was the rector of our parish. He was one of those very kind grandfatherly types who probably could have retired a decade ago but just loved the parish too much to leave. I called and made an appointment.

"Come in, Helen," he said, motioning to the couch in his study. I sat, and he took a seat across from me in an old wooden rocker. I sat there and looked at my shoes. He didn't say anything. I started to cry, weep actually, long, deep convulsions heaving my chest, and tears flowing down my face. Father Tom sat quietly and let me go.

"I don't know what to do," I finally said.

"Do about what?" he said.

"Carly Munroe."

He nodded, waited a moment, and then, "What do you want to do?"

"I want to make it all better."

"Ah, well we all do." He smiled.

"I feel so awful. I wish . . ." I paused for a moment. "I wish it had been me." And I started to cry again.

When I gained partial control, Father Tom said, "Look at me, Helen." He waited for me to stop staring at the floor and when our eyes met he said, "Accidents happen. It's nobody's fault."

"I feel so guilty," I stammered.

"Now that's something we can do something about," he said.

I didn't understand.

"Have you talked with Carly?" he asked.

The idea horrified me. "Talked to her?" I said. "I wouldn't know what to say."

"Yes, you do," he replied quickly.

I thought for a moment. "I need to tell her how sorry I am, don't I?"

"That would be a good beginning," said Father Tom.

"I don't think I can," I said.

"Well," he said, "you're not going to get any better until you do. Forgiveness is what's important. You need to ask for it, and she needs to give it. That's when the healing will begin for both of you."

I thought about that a lot, and finally, after several more sleepless nights, decided that it was time to do what was probably the most difficult thing I would ever do. I went after dinner.

The hospital was quiet when I arrived, and after getting the room number at the information desk, I wandered a bit trying to work up my courage. Finally, I went to Carly's room. I knocked, hoping that she was asleep or maybe not there, but she answered immediately.

I went in. Carly Munroe was in bed and in traction, her legs suspended from a contraption rigged over her bed. Both legs were in casts. She looked at me quizzically.

"Uh, hi," I said, "I'm Helen Manuel."

She nodded silently.

"I came to say," I paused for a moment, "I came to say how sorry I am."

She didn't say anything. I stood there in the dark awkwardness for several minutes and then said, "Well, I won't bother you any more. I'm just so sorry." And I turned to leave.

"You've ruined my life," she said when I was almost to the door. "I was going to be a dancer; I was a dancer; I was good. I had my whole career ahead of me. I was going to go to school in New York next fall on a scholarship. You've ruined it all."

I turned slightly to look at her.

"I never want to see you again," she said. And I was gone.

The next Sunday I told Father Tom what had happened.

"I'm sorry," he said, "but you know you did the right thing."

"It's very painful," I said.

"I can only imagine, Helen, but it's her problem now."

"What?"

"It's Carly's problem."

"What is?"

"She needs to forgive and she won't get any better until she does. Oh, she may walk again, and maybe she'll even dance, but if she can't forgive then she'll be defined by this accident for the rest of her life, and I guarantee it will be a miserable life at that. But you do need to do one more thing for her."

"What's that?" I asked hesitantly.

"You need to pray for her. Every day."

Oddly enough, my encounter with Carly seemed to help in spite of her attitude. I'm sure my praying for her helped too. Oh, it still pained me, and I still cried about it from time to time, but gradually I was able to sleep and eat, and after several months, my life was pretty much normal again.

I even went out and got myself a job. It was the same type of job I had where we previously lived.

"I don't have a spoon!"

I turned around to see Mrs. Joyner pushing her wheelchair back from the table and looking on the floor for the lost utensil. *That's odd*, I thought. I had watched the tables being set an hour ago for lunch, and everyone had had exactly what they were supposed to.

"I don't have a spoon!" said Mrs. Joyner again to no one in particular.

I knelt down next to her, the better to see her eye to eye. "Don't worry, Mrs. Joyner. I'll get you one," I assured her.

This was my second day as program director at the Evergreen Personal Care Facility. It used to be the Evergreen Nursing Home, but even in this rather rural part of the world, the more acceptable designation of "personal care" had arrived. Because I was so new, I was trying to learn everything I could about the operation. Even though I really didn't have anything to do with the serving of meals, I had attended all of them so far just to see how it was done. I could have sworn that there was a spoon there.

I went into the kitchen and retrieved one for Mrs. Joyner.

"Need a spoon?" said a lovely, if overweight, college girl whom I was recently introduced to as Shirley. She was home on break and came back to the facility, where she had volunteered for years. She smiled as she said this, as if she knew something I didn't.

"Helen," a voice sounded behind me, and I turned to see one of the secretaries. "Mr. Dixon would like to see you when you have a moment."

"Who needs the spoon?" said Shirley with another smile.

"Mrs. Joyner," I replied.

Shirley took it from my hand and glided into the dining room with it. I set off down the hall to Herbert Dixon's office.

The facility had been recently built and was state of the art. The rooms were spacious and bright and the amenities top rate. In addition to the elderly whom you would expect to inhabit such a place, there was an entire wing of temporary residents who came to us after serious surgeries. Folks who couldn't be taken care of at home. All of my time, though, was spent trying to keep 120 elderly residents occupied in the sort of activities that exercised their muscles and their minds. There were any number of standard activities that we used. There was toss the balloon, where we would pull the residents into a circle and throw an oversized balloon. There was category, where we would take, for instance, beverages, and see how many the residents could name. And, of course, there was the singing. The residents loved to sing the old songs, and they did so pretty enthusiastically. A typical medley might go from "Amazing Grace" to "I've Been Working on the Railroad" to the "Battle Hymn of the Republic." Early in my career, I learned not to use "The Star Spangled Banner," because they all wanted to stand up, even those who couldn't.

Herbert Dixon was a gregarious and big man who had an unbridled enthusiasm for his work. Even though he was the director of the facility, he spent an immense amount of time out in the halls talking to and greeting patients. "Good morning, Mrs. Marion." "How about that game last night, Mr. Daley?" It was like he was running for office. He always called the residents Mr. or Mrs. unless they insisted otherwise, and he had us do the same. He loved what he did, and he loved these people.

I was standing in front of his desk in his rather sparse office.

"Have a seat, Helen." He gestured to a chair nearby.

"I know you're new here and that we have just gotten past Halloween," he said, and indeed, it was the first week of November, "but I thought I should make you aware of one of the traditions of the facility and the town that you will be responsible for." This sounded a bit ominous to me. "You know, Helen, that Christmas is the major industry in this town, what with all of the tree farms here, and you're aware that on the weekend before Christmas the town has a big pageant."

I nodded. "Little Miss Christmas Tree," I said.

He smiled. "Yes. In fact, Shirley and Joy were the winners last year." I knew Shirley, but I hadn't met Joy yet. I made a mental note of the name.

"Well, on the Saturday afternoon before Christmas, there's another town tradition that has been going on for, oh, maybe thirty or forty years. It's a presentation of the Christmas story by the residents here. "

"Okay," I said, waiting for the other shoe to drop, and it did.

"It started out as a small internal activity, but," and he hesitated just enough to let me know that the bad news was coming, "then it got, well, bigger."

"Bigger?" I asked.

"Yes. At first, some of the family members of the residents came, and then some friends, and well, it just got bigger."

"How much bigger?"

"Uh, pretty much the whole town shows up for it now. It's become a tradition. In fact, when we built this new facility we actually included a stage just to accommodate the pageant."

I must have gone pale.

"Helen, don't worry. You'll have lots of help. In fact, there's a very nice man named Eddie Williams who deals with all the animals."

"All the animals?" I was even paler now.

"Anyway, there's an organizational meeting tomorrow night here."

"And I'm supposed to . . ."

"Organize it," he said. "I'll have the files sent over."

I staggered back to my office, closed the door, and sat down heavily in my chair.

A few minutes later, there was knock on my door, and Shirley Ricketts walked in. She had a stack of file folders that were marked "Celebrate the Miracle."

"Mr. Dixon asked me to drop these by."

"Pageant?" I asked.

"Yeah." She paused in the doorway after handing them to me. "You know, Mrs. Manuel, I've been helping out around here since I was thirteen. If you need any help with anything, or need to know anything . . ."

"Um, thanks," I mumbled, distracted by the folders.

And just before she went out the door, she said, "I know where all the spoons are going."

I followed her into the hall, but she was practically at the end of the corridor by the time I emerged from my office. But she paused, turned, looked at me, and jerked her head to the right as if to say, "Well if you want to know, get down here."

I found myself standing in Mr. McSorley's room, which was empty, as he was at physical therapy. Shirley walked over to the nightstand and slowly opened the drawer to reveal what must have been two hundred metal spoons, all in neat rows, apparently stolen from the dining room.

"Why?" I asked.

"Who knows," said Shirley. "The funny thing is he takes one and only one every lunch, and it's always a clean one. Joy and I stumbled on it last summer, and it's gotten to be sort of a game to see when the nursing staff or dining staff figure it out."

"Shouldn't they be returned?"

"Well, we figured it was harmless enough, and you know, it seems to give him some meaning, something to do, and you know, it's kind of funny. The guy's ninety-five, has Alzheimer's, and moves like molasses, but he's managed to steal a spoon every lunchtime for maybe nine months and not get caught. I sort of admire him for it. You won't tell, will you?"

There was something about this girl I liked, something that said she could be trusted. "Tell me what you know about the pageant," I said.

"Come with me," she said.

We walked into the dayroom, where there were several residents watching TV and a woman I had not seen before. She was clutching a baby doll.

"I have to help Mrs. Ferguson," Shirley said. Mrs. Ferguson evoked a sadness in me that was almost indescribable. Shirley told me what she knew. Apparently, Mrs. Ferguson hadn't spoken in nearly ten years. When her children brought her to the home she was carrying the doll, and when anyone tried to take it from her she experienced so much anxiety that the staff thought she might hurt herself. Shirley said she just sat all day, every day, holding the doll and staring at the floor. Sometimes, she wandered up and down the hall, but she was completely withdrawn and uncommunicative. Shirley had discovered that Mrs. Ferguson liked ice cream, and it became a ritual that after lunch she took her to the dayroom and fed her dessert.

So while Shirley fed Mrs. Ferguson, she told me about the pageant. "Actually," she said, "it's not that hard to do. It's one of those events that people have been doing for so long that it pretty much runs itself. The same people do the props and the lighting and the directing and so forth; the only problem is," she hesitated.

"What?" I asked.

"Well, the really big deal is the casting."

"The casting?"

"Yeah, the show is such a big deal now, and the whole town shows up for the performance. The competition for the key roles is pretty fierce. Especially for Mary. There are residents who don't talk to each other anymore over who was cast as Mary or Joseph or even the angel."

"Really?"

"Yep, and since the casting is your responsibility, you can expect the lobbying to begin at any moment."

"Lobbying?"

"Oh yeah, there will be certain residents who will try to get close just so they can have a key part. In fact, one year, a certain Mrs. Smithton tried to get herself admitted to the home in November with the hope that she would get the part of Mary. Another year, your predecessor found a hundred dollar bill in a Christmas card from Mr. Nolan, who wanted to be Gabriel."

I felt a migraine coming on.

The next morning, it started. There was a knock on my door, and Mrs. Conley hobbled in on her walker. She managed to carry a small bouquet of carnations that she either bought in the gift shop or stole from the dining room tables; I wasn't sure.

"I wanted to say welcome," she said, handing me the flowers.

"Thank you," I said.

"Well, if you need any help with anything . . ." She paused, as if her words had some hidden meaning that I would surely understand.

She smiled sweetly. "I once played Stella."

"Stella?" I asked, confused.

"You know, Stella Kowalski?"

"Ah," I said, "*A Streetcar Named Desire.*"

"Yes, and I was very good. I have clippings." She began to rummage through the pockets of her immense housedress. "One reviewer said I was better than Kim Hunter and prettier, too." She winked at me.

She handed me a yellowed news clipping from the *Tyrone County Weekly Examiner*. Which indeed did praise her work at the local community theater forty years ago.

"How nice," I managed.

"So," she plowed ahead, "playing Mary would not be a problem," and she winked again.

I suppressed a laugh as the idea of Stella Kowalski playing the Virgin Mary struck me as funny.

"Well, I'll keep that in mind," I said, showing her the door.

Mrs. Conley was just the first. Mrs. Kucinich, Mrs. Retzer, and Mrs. Harper all wanted to be Mary and let me know it that day. Mrs. Harper offered me a two-for-one, as her husband was also a resident, and she claimed he would make a dandy Joseph. Mr. Carlisle stopped me at lunch to say he didn't have a spoon, and when I brought one to him asked if he might play Gabriel. This led to a guffaw from his tablemate Mr. Quinn, who claimed that there weren't, as he put it, "any boy angels."

"Idiot," Mr. Carlisle intoned, shaking his head. And then there was Mrs. Allen, who wanted to play Gabriel because, she claimed, she often saw angels and knew exactly how they behaved.

In the end, I decided to do what any quality production would do, and that was hold auditions. I was smart enough not to do it all by myself and invited Andy Harper, who was directing the show, and a couple other staff to help. It took an entire day, and a very amusing one at that. I hadn't thought, until then, of the visual effect of having many actors who were in wheelchairs or using walkers cast as biblical characters. This was going to be quite a show.

As it turned out, Mrs. Conley, aka Stella Kowalski, *was* cast as Mary. She apparently had the same chops in old age that she did in her twenties. Unfortunately, she hadn't lost any of her apparent tendencies toward being a prima donna, and I caught her on several occasions inserting into dinner conversations the fact that *she* had been cast as Mary, and by the way did you know I played Stella in *Street Car*? It did not endear her to the other residents, especially those who wanted the part themselves. I even found her one afternoon going over her lines in front of Mrs. Ferguson, who was mutely clutching her doll, apparently oblivious to the quality acting before her.

The new job, the geriatric pageant, and the approaching holidays mostly took my mind from last summer's accident. I wondered from time to time how Carly was doing, if she was getting better. If she would ever dance again. I also found myself praying for her like Father Tom told me to. Mostly, I just prayed for her to be healed. Now, while I wasn't thinking of this specifically, I guess what I was really praying for was a miracle, and that's what I got. Actually I got three.

The Saturday before Christmas arrived, and the pageant performance was to take place late that afternoon. People began to arrive an hour early. By four o'clock, the auditorium was full. I didn't get a seat, and so Shirley and I stood against a wall to watch. Standing Room Only.

The lights dimmed, and Mr. Feinstein began the narration. Mr. Anderson, dressed in camel hair and clutching his walker, entered the stage as John the Baptist and admonished everyone to repent. He was really into it and was actually quite good. Then the story went back to the announcement of Jesus's birth. Mrs. Conley dressed in a blue robe portraying Mary and Mr. Carlisle as Gabriel took the center stage. The spotlight fell on the two of them, and Mr. Carlisle rendered his lines flawlessly: ". . . and of his Kingdom there shall be no end." He finished in his best angelic voice, and then . . . silence.

Mrs. Conley looked like a statue. She was supposed to have the next line, but didn't move. Out of the corner of my eye, I noticed something moving in the center aisle.

"How shall this be . . ." I heard someone whisper loudly from the wings.

Nothing.

"How shall this be . . ." came the whisper again.

I was trying to make out who was walking up the aisle.

"How shall this be . . ." blurted Mrs. Conley flatly, and then, nothing.

Something told me that Mrs. Conley wasn't going to be carrying clippings about *this* performance in her housecoat.

Mr. Carlisle went to his next line, and it looked like it was going to be okay. It was time for Mrs. Conley to recite the Magnificat. She had been doing it for weeks. Boring the other residents to tears with it. Now, silence. Apparently, Mrs. Conley was in the throes of some very significant stage fright.

There was a set of steps in front of the stage, and the figure in the aisle began to slowly climb them. Mr. Carlisle tried not to look, but his face couldn't help but reflect shock and surprise. As she entered the light, I could finally see that it was Mrs. Ferguson, clutching her baby doll. *This is not good*, I said to myself. One of the nurse's aids started up the aisle toward the stage, but then Mr. Dixon, for some unknown reason, waved her off.

Mrs. Ferguson silently walked over to the dumbstruck Virgin Mary and handed her the baby doll. Then she turned dead in the center of the follow spot, looked out at the audience, and said, "My soul doth magnify the Lord and my spirit rejoices in God my saviour." And she did the whole speech without a hesitation, without a stop, without a missed word. She did it perfectly. And then, leaving the baby with Mary, she quietly returned to her seat.

I have never been in a room so silent in all my life. Not a sound, not a stirring, and I couldn't help myself. "It's a miracle," I whispered, but in that hushed environment the words thundered, and the audience turned to look at me, and there in the middle of everyone, sitting in a wheelchair, was Carly Munroe. Our eyes met and then she looked away. The pieces fell together; she must be a patient on the rehab wing. Here we were in the same building every day, and neither of us knew it.

Mrs. Ferguson's performance seemed to inspire Mrs. Conley who, in spite of having a baby delivered to her three scenes too soon, launched into her next lines with all of the professionalism of someone lauded by the *Tyrone County Weekly Examiner* for her realistic portrayal of Stella Kowalski.

The rest of the play went off rather nicely, and then it was time for the wise men to appear. Mr. McSorley, Mr. Richards, and Mr. Hubert were Gold, Frankincense, and Myrrh, respectively, and Mr. McSorley led the way down the center aisle while the choir sang "We Three Kings." Mr. Richards and Mr. Hubert were carrying their fancy box and bottle, but Mr. McSorley was carrying something much larger and obviously heavier than I had seen in rehearsal. When he got to the steps, I knew what he had. How a ninety-five-year-old man with Alzheimer's could carry a drawer filled with forty pounds of spoons, I'll never know. But he lugged them up the stairs and laid them at the foot of the manger with as much pomp and ceremony as if he had gold bullion.

Shirley Ricketts leaned over to me, saying "Looks like another miracle," and we both giggled.

The curtain went down, the applause went up, and an hour later everyone was pretty much back to normal. I went to my office and sat down behind my desk. I didn't realize how tired I was. My eyes fell to the pageant folder on my desk and the title "Celebrate the Miracle." I couldn't help but smile.

Then I was aware that there was someone in the doorway.

"I didn't mean to startle you," Carly Munroe said from her wheelchair.

I got up from my desk. "Won't you come in?" I said nervously.

Carly wheeled her chair through the doorway, and I sat down in the side chair along the wall. We were both quiet for a moment.

"How are you, Carly?"

"Well, they say that with a lot of work I'm going to walk again."

"That's good."

"I suppose. There's even a chance that I might dance again someday."

"I'm glad to hear that."

Carly was staring at the floor. I could tell she had something she wanted to say.

"That was quite a show," she finally said.

"Yes, it was," I agreed.

"You know Mrs. Ferguson? The lady with the baby doll?" asked Carly.

"Yes."

"She's my grandmother." She paused. "Ever watch someone you love lose their mind?"

"No," I said.

"It's horrible," she said. "I can remember when I was little my grandmother was funny and vibrant. She baked cookies and did all the stuff that grandmothers do. And then she just started to lose her mind. At first it was just forgetfulness, but within a couple of years, she was completely silent. The doll she has . . ."

I nodded.

"It was mine. It was the only thing that seemed to pacify her. I haven't seen her without it or heard her speak in almost ten years. And then tonight . . ." a tear appeared in the corner of her eye, "and then tonight she not only spoke but," she was crying a little harder now, "but she gave it up."

Carly fairly dissolved into tears. I handed her a box of tissues.

"You know," she went on after she regained her composure, "I used to believe in miracles. I used to believe in a god who loved me and the Christmas thing. But then I had the accident, and I knew that God wasn't real, or if he was, he was some sort of cruel god who liked to torment people. It didn't make any sense that this would happen to me."

"I know what you mean," I said.

"I believe in miracles now," said Carly. "And the funny thing is that it's more than you know because my grandmother spoke to me tonight from that stage, and you know what I heard her say?"

"No."

"I heard her say, 'Give it up, Carly.' I heard her say, 'You can hang on to the hurt and resentment and anger and be miserable the rest of your life, or you can give it up. It's your choice, but I'm your grandmother, and I love you enough to tell you it's time to give it up.'"

Now I was crying.

Carly went on, "I treated you horribly in the hospital. I wanted to hurt you like you hurt me. But the funny thing was it was more like stabbing myself than you. So I knew I needed to come over here and tell you," she paused to wipe away another tear, "to tell you that I forgive you, and that I'm sorry, too."

I got up from my chair and walked over to her and put my arms around her, and we both cried.

"It's going to be okay," I said. "You're forgiven." aA then I said, "You only know half of it," and I told her about Mr. McSorley and the spoons, and we laughed long and hard.

Miracles do happen. I saw a bunch of them that night. I saw the miracle of a catatonic grandmother speak for the first time in a decade and tell her granddaughter she loved her. I saw the miracle of a ninety-five-year-old man return his purloined spoon collection without being asked, and that might have been enough for one night. But the best was yet to come.

When most of us think about miracles we think about the Red Sea parting or water turning into wine or five thousand fed with a few loaves, and as impressive as those are, there are greater miracles. The greatest miracle I experienced that night wasn't Mr. McSorley or Mrs. Ferguson; it was Carly Munroe. Because it was Carly Munroe who brought me the miracle of forgiveness. It is an amazing thing if you stop to think about it: that we can make such messes or be involved in such horrific accidents and be forgiven.

But I also knew that all of this was not separate from what we had been celebrating that evening. That among the shepherds and angels, wise men and sheep, there was a baby. That it was the baby, Jesus, who made the forgiveness possible. I knew that it was only because of his death and resurrection that forgiveness was possible, and that could only happen because he came to earth to be one of us.

And so Carly and I believe in miracles again, miracles of love and forgiveness, and the miracle of Jesus Christ.

7

ST. MICHAEL

This is a story that is completely explainable, but when it's told it may also be unbelievable. As I look back on the events of that Christmas Eve, all of it makes sense. I mean, I don't think there really was anything supernatural but . . .

Let me start at the beginning and the beginning is at the church. My wife, Sarah, is part of the Christian Education Committee at St. Mary's and that group is charged with, among other items, the annual Christmas pageant. This has always been performed by the children. I'm sure you've seen one before. A lot of little children dressed in bedsheets, which, depending on how they get wrapped, means they are either angels or shepherds—the shepherds also being distinguished by the towels wrapped around their heads with yarn. The older children play the characters with speaking parts: Mary, Joseph, the innkeeper, the angels. The kids work hard at memorizing their lines and most of them do a pretty good job. It's hard to miss with kids, although last year's pageant did border on disaster. It has been referred to as the "Christmas Pageant from Hell."

The MacNamara twins, age eight, were part of the heavenly host, but apparently against their will. During the Gloria in Excelsis they got into a shoving match that resulted in little Marion

Kelly getting pushed into the manger, sending baby Jesus, played by a Cabbage Patch Kid, sliding across the sanctuary floor. At that moment Amber Geringer, who was playing Mary and who, unbeknownst to anyone, was in the early stages of a forty-eight-hour flu, got sick on Joseph. Joseph screamed, sending twelve tiny preschool angels flying down the aisles in search of their parents. One of them tripped over an electric cord, causing a six-foot stand of stage lights to come crashing down. This, of course, dispersed the rest of the cast and brought the entire production to a swift conclusion.

After a short break to clean up, make sure no one was hurt, and get everyone settled, Father Elston said that that would be a tough act to follow but he would try. And with a mixture of emotions we had Communion, sang "Silent Night," and all went home to await with fear and trepidation next year's pageant.

Father Elston approached the whole situation with a fair amount of humor, but he did let the Christian Education Committee know that something different had to happen next year—otherwise, he said, they might be sued for risking a catastrophe. The committee complied with a novel idea.

My wife, Sarah, came home from the October meeting and made the announcement. This year the pageant would be done by the adults.

"Adults?" I said somewhat incredulously. "Do you really think that you can get a group of adults to dress up and act all of that out?"

"Michael," she said with that tone that let me know that a little more support on my part would be greatly appreciated, "this is a wonderful idea. We can show the children that Christmas is for adults too and that the pageant is important. We can model for them what a pageant can look like and the following year they will have that in mind when they do it again."

"I'm skeptical," I said.

"So what else is new?" she sneered, as she went up the stairs to get ready for bed.

I sat in the chair in the darkened living room and listened to the noises of my wife upstairs. I was in my pajamas—I'd been in them all day. In fact, I hadn't been properly dressed or out of the house in a month. I was a mess. I wasn't in the mood to be thinking about Christmas, or pageants, or children, especially not about children. I guess I should explain.

When I was twelve my best friend was Jack Dandridge. We were inseparable. We had known each other since kindergarten and had done everything together for the following seven years. We were in Scouts together, I pitched for our Little League team and Jack was the catcher, and I even went with his family on vacation up at the lake.

One Friday in December, I was spending the night at his house and we awoke in the darkness and smelled smoke. The house was on fire. We jumped from our beds and made for the door of his room. We opened it to find the hallway fully ablaze. Thick black smoke poured into the room. Jack began to cry. I crossed the room and tried to open the window, but it was painted shut. I couldn't open it. The smoke was getting thicker. We were coughing and could barely keep our eyes open. I don't know what possessed me to keep my head, but I picked up a chair and I threw it at the window. The glass shattered all around. I grabbed a pillow and used it to clear the broken shards from around the frame. I stuck my head out and breathed the fresh air. Looking down I could see that it was about a thirty-foot drop to the ground. The fire was in the room now. Jack was paralyzed. I dragged him to the window.

"We're going to have to jump!" I yelled. Something crashed in the house and I could hear sirens in the distance. "Jack, we're going to have to jump!"

"I can't," he whimpered.

"We don't have a choice," I said. The heat was enormous. "Come on, we'll go together. Hold my hand."

Jack was dazed. I made him sit on the windowsill with me and we held hands. "It'll be okay," I said. "Just hang on to my hand."

As I jumped, I was only vaguely aware that Jack had let go of my hand.

I awoke in the hospital with a broken leg, cracked ribs, and a concussion. My parents were there to tell me that Jack had died in the fire. A neighbor had witnessed my trying to help Jack get out, and in the midst of their tears and sorrow, Mom and Dad told me how proud they were of me. But it was little comfort. Before I left the hospital I had decided what it was that I would do with my life.

I stopped playing ball and stopped going to Scouts. Every spare minute I had, I spent at the firehouse. The firemen all knew who I was because they had been there that night. They were wonderfully kind. I helped to wash the trucks and clean the equipment. I learned how all the equipment worked, and when I was a teenager my parents gave permission for me to ride with the trucks to the fires—where I stayed out of the way and helped behind the scenes where I could.

By the time I was twenty-five I had graduated from the fire academy and was hired by the city. I would redeem that awful night. I did well as a firefighter. I knew what I was doing and I took few risks. One day I even had my picture on the front page of the morning paper running from a burning apartment building with a baby in my arms. They gave me a medal. But in spite of the accolades and promotions, I still needed to do something. I just didn't know what.

Last month, we had a three-alarm fire at a residence. We got there in time to keep the house from being totally gutted, but the family lost all five of their children to smoke. I found them huddled in a closet. I snapped. I just stood there unable to move, unable to feel, unable to think. They had to take me to the hospital, where I stayed for a week. I've been home ever since. I thought that I had put Jack's death behind me, that I was working that through with my job. I believed that if I was diligent at it that I could keep people from dying. But then these children died and there was no reason. There was nothing I could do. I didn't want to work anymore. I didn't want to do anything. I talked to doctors and shrinks. Father Elston even came to the house several times.

That was remarkable, since my church attendance had been erratic at best. He's a good man. He just wasn't much help.

How can anyone believe in a god when things like this happen? How can anyone have joy when innocent children get killed? I was a mess.

Sarah was supportive. She pushed gently and cared for me. She didn't pamper me, but made me be responsible. Eventually, by Thanksgiving, I had returned to a desk job with the department. I was still incredibly depressed and terribly skeptical about the world. I refused to go to church with her.

"Michael, you can't just turn your back on God," she said.

"What's God ever done for me?" I responded.

"You're alive, aren't you? Think of all the stuff you've been through. And I'm not just talking about when you were twelve. Think of all the people you've saved, the child you rescued that time. God must be with you."

"I'd rather he had been with Jack or those kids."

"Look, I don't know why those things happen. No one does. What I know is you're alive and you had better not waste that gift."

I was unconvinced.

Sarah was undeterred by my negativity and set about to make sure that this year's pageant was a success. She found a group of adults who were not only willing to do the pageant, but who were excited about the possibility. She cast herself as Mary.

Because adults were involved, the whole pageant became much more complex, with extensive lines to be learned. Sarah convinced me to help her with her part, and in spite of my emotional condition, I figured I owed her at least that much. So we spent almost every evening in December going over her lines, with me reading the other parts. I even managed to attend the dress rehearsal a couple days before the Christmas Eve presentation. I have to say I was impressed. The costumes were glorious, the staging looked professional, the props were realistic, and in spite of their amateur status, the actors did a rather commendable job. I even agreed to come to church that evening and witness the spectacle.

At about four o'clock on Christmas Eve the phone rang. Sarah answered and a short conversation ensued. She then came into the living room. She was ashen.

"What's wrong?" I asked.

She slumped into a chair. "That was Hank Appling's wife. Hank was called to the hospital for some kind of emergency surgery."

"So?"

"So? Hank was supposed to play Gabriel and I don't have anybody to fill in for him. The pageant's going to be ruined." She put her face in her hands and began to cry.

I sat there and watched her. I wanted to put my arms around her but I couldn't. I didn't have it in me. She was completely gone. This thing that she had worked so hard for was about to fall apart.

"Don't worry. It'll work out," I said, playing the improbable role of the optimist.

"Oh yeah—right. It starts in three hours. How am I . . . where am I going to find . . . ." She started to cry again.

And then, from some dark and seldom lit part of myself, came the most unpredictable and surprising words. "I'll do it," I said.

She stopped crying immediately at the unexpectedness of my response. She looked at me with that beautiful face, red and blotchy from tears. "You'd really do that?"

"Sure," I said, feeling less and less sure all the time. "I know the lines, I saw the dress rehearsal . . ."

"Oh, I don't know."

"What other choice do you have?"

We both got up and hugged for the first time in a long time.

Hank Appling's costume was at the church and I found it when we arrived. It consisted of a long white robe onto which had been sewn some pretty elaborate wings. I put it on.

"Michael, really," my wife said, looking at my feet.

"What?"

"You look like an angel from Brooks Brothers with those pants and shoes."

Sure enough, the last six inches of my pants were showing, as well as my black wing-tipped shoes. Hank Appling, I learned, was a lot shorter than I was.

"Now what?" I asked.

"Take off your pants," my wife replied.

"I beg your pardon?"

"Michael, you can't go out there like that. No one will be able to tell you don't have pants on. Just do it in bare feet."

I was skeptical about this, but had come too far to turn back, so I dutifully removed my shoes and socks and trousers.

"That's better," pronounced my wife.

The pageant itself went off without a hitch except that baby Jesus, who was being played by two-month-old Brenda Thomas, spit up on Joseph, but I figured it probably happened that way in real life anyway.

I had told Sarah that I wasn't going to stay for the rest of the service, so when we were done I made my way back to the parish hall. We had come in separate cars, and I planned on meeting her back at the house. What I didn't count on was that we had gotten dressed in the choir room, which was in a building on the other side of the sanctuary. I couldn't get to it without either going through the sanctuary or going outside in the snow. I decided to wait. I found a lounge in the parish house and sat on the couch. I didn't turn on any lights. My wings made it hard to sit, and I found that the only way I could be comfortable was to either stand or lie on my stomach on the couch. I chose the latter and promptly fell asleep.

When I awoke I had no idea what time it was. Everything was dark. I walked the black halls wondering where everyone was. I came to the sanctuary door and listened. Nothing. I slowly opened it to find it dark and empty. I stumbled across the nave and found the door to the choir room. It was locked. *Great*, I thought. I traveled back the way I had come. I'd have to call Sarah and have her come rescue me, but the door leading back from where I had come had locked behind me.

I thought for a minute. I was getting angrier all the time. I decided on the only option left to me. I exited the sanctuary to the outside to get my truck. There were about two feet of snow, although the temperature was hardly below freezing. Still, my feet were aching from the cold when I got to the truck and retrieved the spare key from under the bumper. I had a little trouble getting in with my wings—they kept catching on the door frame. Sitting in the seat was even more difficult, but I finally managed a position that didn't seem to be life-threatening and started the engine.

I pulled out of the lot and started home. *Boy, Sarah owes me big this time*, I thought. *How could she just leave me there? Surely she must have seen my truck. Just wait till I get home!*

The Logan County Road from St. Mary's to our house is lonely and deserted. We hardly see any traffic on it. Even at this hour (whatever hour it was) and in spite of my condition, I was struck by how beautiful and peaceful everything seemed under this blanket of snow illuminated by the moon. I was feeling a little better now. The heater in the truck was working and I was looking forward to bed. That's when I saw him.

There was this kid, maybe twelve years old, standing in the middle of the road waving his hands. Pulled off to the side of the road was a red minivan.

I pulled up behind the van and opened the truck door. I nearly strangled myself as my wings got caught in the shoulder harness, but I finally got myself untangled to find this boy standing in front of me. For some reason he was very wide eyed and his mouth was hanging open.

"What's wrong, kid?" I asked.

He just stared for a moment and then remembering what was happening said, "It's my mom." He led me around to the sliding door of the van, and on opening it I was confronted with a woman in her midthirties who was very pregnant.

"Oh, thank God," she cried. "I'm having a baby."

"Just relax," I said. "I'll drive you to the hospital."

"You don't understand; I'm having it right now," she said with her face contorted and she started to breath in those short breaths they teach you at childbirth classes.

I felt dizzy. I backed away and ran to my truck, my bare feet slipping on the snow-packed road. I tuned my two-way radio to the emergency channel and called for an ambulance—but I knew the hospital was a good twenty-five minutes away.

I slid back to the van and, climbing into the back, folded down the rear seat to form a small bed. I got the lady to lie back there with her head propped against the side window. She was having another contraction now.

"Don't worry," I lied. "I've done this before."

Actually, I had been trained to do this, but had never actually been a part of one of these before. I wasn't going to let her know how scared I was—she looked scared enough already.

And so, I delivered a baby.

It's strange what goes through your mind during a crisis. While I was yelling "push" and hoping everything was all right, I could see myself. I was jumping—jumping from a window into the darkness. I started to fall and I fell for the longest time. I could see Jack in his Little League uniform, smiling behind the plate. I could see him waving to me from that green canoe on the lake. I could see a family sitting at the dinner table, five children holding hands and saying grace. I could see a woman giving birth to a child—a woman who wasn't in a hospital or even in a minivan parked on a country road, but rather a woman in a barn. And there was an angel, and the angel was saying, "Behold! I bring good tidings of great joy, for unto you is born a Savior who is Christ the King." And then the father, who had been sitting at the table with the children, got up and walked over to me. He put his arms around me and said, "Mike, it'll be okay. I love you."

Now I looked in my hands and there was a child screaming and crying. There was a woman I didn't even know and she was crying great tears of joy. And I was crying, too.

I could hear sirens in the distance as I handed the baby to the mother and got out of the van. Headlights far down the road were drawing nearer.

Then I suddenly remembered that I was dressed like a barefoot angel. These guys in the ambulance would know me. I'd never hear the end of it. I started for the truck.

"Hey!" someone shouted.

I turned around. It was the kid.

"Where are you going?"

I walked back to him. "I've got to go. You know, it's Christmas. This is a busy time for me."

"Are you really an angel?" he asked.

And then, for some reason I don't quite understand, I said, "Always remember this night and remember how much God loves you."

Then I turned.

"Hey, wait. What's your name?" the boy asked.

"Michael," I said, and then I drove away.

When I got home, Sarah was worried and waiting. I started to tell her about what had just happened and then stopped. I simply said that I had fallen asleep in the lounge and awoken to find everyone gone. She took appropriate pity on me and we went to bed.

Even though the next day was Christmas, I slept in, but I was awakened by my wife, who jumped on the bed with the newspaper.

"Hey!" she said.

"Hey, yourself." I managed squinting at her.

"Want to hear something curious?" She had that wry smile she has when she knows something important that you don't.

"Okay," I said gamely.

She began to read from the front page of the paper.

"Archangel Michael Delivers Baby." "A Middletown woman told paramedics that when she went into labor driving her minivan on Logan County Road last night, an angel came and delivered her. Megan Norris claims that an angel, who stated that he had done this before, found her and her twelve-year-old son and delivered her baby. The angel, who said his name was Michael, was about six feet, four inches with sandy hair and blue eyes. He was driving a red pickup truck. Paramedics arrived to find the healthy seven pound, five ounce baby boy, his mother, and brother *alone* in the van. The Norris's have decided to name the child Michael after their heavenly obstetrician. . . ." There was more.

Sarah looked up. "Is there anything you want to tell me?"

"Yeah," I said. "Stop buying those tabloids in the checkout line." She hit me with a pillow.

I did tell her the whole story and we laughed and cried. But something more and indescribable—something deeper—had happened. Somehow something got fixed. In the midst of all the doubts and darkness, life had won and I was back. It took the birth of a child to do that. Actually it took the birth of two children. One was born in a minivan with the assistance of a wayward and skeptical angel.

But the first was born long ago in a stable. The angels there were real and were right about the good news. The good news of a father who wraps us in his arms, who whispers his love in our ear, and who sometimes takes us home.

8

COMFORT AND JOY

I have a love-hate relationship with my hair. Actually, it's more of a hate-hate relationship.

My parents told me that when I was born, I was as bald as a billiard ball, and for months I had no hair. In fact, they were worried that I had some condition that would leave me permanently bald. But eventually, the hair began to grow and when it did it was bright red.

This was the source of endless speculation in our family, because no one knew of even a distant relative with red hair.

When I was six, my baby sister was baptized. The minister, a very jolly and outgoing man, had our family come forward, and he looked at me and said, "My goodness, Evelyn, where did you get all that red hair?"

I looked him dead in the eye and said, loudly enough so that the entire congregation could hear, "The mailman."

The minister went pale and the entire congregation, much to my dismay, burst into laughter. Of course, I didn't get the joke; I was only repeating what I had heard others say. I guess I thought my parents had ordered my hair through a catalog and the mailman delivered it.

When I was twelve, I was at the grocery store with my mom, and a woman I'd never seen commented on my hair.

"What, exactly, is that color?" she asked somewhat derisively.

"Red," I said.

"Well," she replied, "I guess it's better than being bald." She had no idea how prophetic she was being.

I hated my hair.

I was born and raised in the small town of Evergreen. It's one of those picturesque rural villages that looks a bit like it fell off a postcard. Its primary business was Christmas. There were no fewer than twelve Christmas tree farms in the area, and the town was filled with small shops that traded almost exclusively in Christmas-themed merchandise. It was a busy place in December, but also in the summer when the town would host the "Christmas in July" festival on the twenty-fifth, complete with a parade and a visit from a vacationing Santa.

But of course, it's December when we pull out all of the stops, and it seems like every weekend in that month there is something special going on. Probably the highlight is the community pageant. It's a very big production with anyone in the town who wants to participate. Some years, it gets so big that people joke that there's no one left in town to be the audience.

While anybody can be a shepherd or an angel, there is a pretty fierce competition for the major roles. Typically, veterans of previous performances are rewarded with the beefier parts. I've been in it ever since I can remember.

Rehearsals start in the fall, but the parts are cast in July. This was to be my year. I was cast as Mary. It's difficult to explain what a big deal this is. There's always a lot of cattiness among the women in town over this, and I was thrilled to finally have hit the "big time." After years of smaller parts, I was going to be the star.

In August, I started to not feel very well. I couldn't quite identify the problem, but I was constantly fatigued. I had no energy. I finally felt bad enough that I went, reluctantly, to my doctor. She ordered a battery of tests, and several days later, I got a call from her office. They wanted to see me immediately. I knew that couldn't be good.

I went down to the office and was escorted into an examination room. I sat for a while on the cushioned table with that stiff white paper on it, and finally, after what seemed like an eternity, Dr. Barrows came in. She stood in front of me for a moment staring at her shoes with her hands in the pockets of her lab coat. Then she looked up and said, "Well, Evelyn, there's no easy way to say this, but you have cancer." She paused for a moment to let the news sink in.

When I heard the word *cancer*, everything went into slow motion, and I couldn't move. *It couldn't possibly be true*, I thought. *I exercise, watch what I eat, and don't smoke. How could this happen? It must be some sort of mistake.*

I couldn't speak, and then Dr. Barrows, as if she were reading my mind, said, "It's not a mistake Evelyn, and I know what a shock this is, but we need to schedule you for surgery right away to see how extensive it is. The good news is that if you had to have cancer, this is what you'd want. It's very treatable, and if it hasn't spread, the survival rate is extremely high."

You never know how some shocking news, news that will change your life forever, will affect you. Or what you might say in response, and it seems incredible to me, but after I had absorbed the news, I looked at Dr. Barrows and said, "But I'm supposed to be Mary in the pageant."

Can you believe that? I'm facing the possibility of a terminal disease, and I'm worried about my starring role in the pageant.

She looked at me in disbelief, and when I realized how ridiculous this must have sounded, I began to laugh and she laughed, too, but the tears would come soon enough.

I decided that, for the time being, I was only going to tell my husband. I wanted to know how bad it was before telling anyone else. The surgery was scheduled for a few days later, and I was just there overnight and another appointment with the doctor was scheduled. I found myself sitting on the same table, but this time my husband, Tom, was standing next to me holding my hand.

The minute Dr. Barrows walked into the room, I knew it was going to be good news.

"Well, Evelyn," she said with a smile, "the report is back, and it's pretty good news."

"Oh?" I managed.

"The cancer hasn't spread, and it looks like the surgeon got what was there. But, to make sure it's all gone, we're going to have to have you do chemotherapy."

"So sort of a good-news-bad-news scenario?"

"Well, yes. Think of the chemo as a push broom that sweeps away any cancer cells that might remain."

"Oh, okay."

It was a bit more complicated than this, but I met with my oncologist, who prescribed a particular regimen for me based on the type of cancer and its severity. As we were talking he said, "You might want to go wig shopping now."

"Wig shopping?"

"Well, yes, you're going to lose your hair during this process."

More good news.

There was no place in Evergreen that sold wigs, so my friend Christine and I drove forty miles to a shop that specializes in such things. We walked through the door and were met by a very pleas-ant saleswoman.

She asked if she could help, and I told her the story, which she undoubtedly had heard a thousand times before.

"Can you match my color?" I asked.

"Well, um," she stammered, "what color is that?" And then she very quickly added, "I'm so sorry. That came out wrong."

"Don't worry," I replied. "I get that a lot."

Of course, they didn't have anything close to my color, but it could be special ordered and was very expensive. Christine and I had fun trying on wigs and saying things like, "Look, I'm Marilyn

Monroe" or "Oh my goodness, you look like Harpo Marx." I decided to put my vanity aside and look like Mr. Clean.

I didn't know it, but I was becoming depressed. Not "I need drugs" depressed, but my attitude and outlook were pretty low. What we sometimes call "blue."

I went for my first chemo. It would take several hours to administer, and Tom took me and sat in the waiting room. I sat down in what I would later refer to as "my big comfy chair." I was hooked up, and the chemo began.

There were other chairs in the room, all of them empty, but about a half hour into my treatment, a woman was escorted into the room. She was as bald as an egg.

She plopped down in a chair, obviously a pro at this, and said to the nurse, "Hook me up, Sheila. I'm ready to roll!" But she said it like she was about to receive some great gift. She looked over at me and smiled.

"First time?"

"Yeah," I replied.

"Nothing to it," she said optimistically. "You'll be fine."

She introduced herself as Lola Townsend, and we chatted during our treatments about kids and family—the sorts of stuff you talk about when you first meet each other.

My treatment ended, and I said goodbye to Lola. Tom took me home, and I threw up for two days. I was getting sadder.

I went back the next week, and Lola was there, and we chatted. Same sickness after that one, only several days later, I noticed my hair was coming out in little bunches.

After the third treatment, it was coming out faster. I was standing in the bathroom looking at myself in the mirror, and I looked terrible. I was pale and drawn, and the hair that I hated was now patchy and ugly.

"I don't deserve this," I said out loud, and I began to cry. After several minutes of sobbing, I dried my eyes and looked back at this person in the mirror I barely recognized.

"Tom!" I called out.

Tom came racing up the stairs thinking that something was wrong.

He was standing in the doorway looking at me looking in the mirror.

"What is it, honey?" he asked with great concern.

I continued to look in the mirror and said, "Tom, get a razor."

It didn't take long, and he was so gentle there wasn't even a nick. But I was completely and utterly bald.

I looked in the mirror and began to cry again.

"Hey," said Tom, and he took me by the shoulders and turned me gently to face him, and then he put his arms around me, and said, "In sickness and in health."

And I responded, "To love and to cherish."

We both knew the next line, which went unsaid: "Until we are parted by death."

At my next treatment, Lola walked in, took one look at me, smiled, and said, "You look great." She plopped down in her chair.

"Oh, please, Lola," I said, "how can you say that?"

Sheila the nurse started to hook my friend up, and Lola said, "No, really, it makes your eyes look so bright." And then she added, "You know, God only made so many perfect heads and on the rest he put hair."

Even I couldn't resist smiling at this.

Maybe it was the joke, or maybe something deeper, but we sat in silence a moment, and I said to Lola, "Do you believe in God?"

She paused a moment, and then responded, "I wouldn't be here if I didn't."

"I'm sorry?" I said.

"Evy," she said, "this is the second time around with this for me. I beat it six years ago, and it came back with a vengeance. It was terrifying, and I was very angry. I told myself I didn't deserve this."

"Well, you don't," I said.

She went on. "In the midst of my anger, a friend said something to me that I'll never forget. She said, 'Lola, you can either go through this with rage, or you can go through this with joy, and frankly joy is a better look on you.'"

"How?" I asked.

"Well, I figured the only place I could go to find that joy was God. It wasn't a quick fix. It took time, but what I started to do was to literally count my blessings. Kids, friends, husband, home, the list went on and on and on, and after a while, I realized that what I'd been blessed with was far greater than the disease I had. It's ironic, but the cancer made me joyful."

"But what if you die?"

"Evy, I don't want to be flip, but we're all going to die. The question is: What do you do with the time you have? Do you spend it in self-pity and anger, or do you go another direction? I'm not afraid to die. I know who I belong to, and I know he watches over me and will bring me home when it's time."

She paused for a moment, and then she said, "Evelyn."

I looked over at her.

She said, "Sometimes you have to lose something before you realize how blessed you are." And then she added, "Comfort and joy."

Comfort and joy.

And so that's what I tried to do, but it wasn't easy. I just couldn't see what it was that I had to be joyful about when I was dealing with cancer. I couldn't understand how my losing was going to show me a blessing. I couldn't find that comfort and joy.

Rehearsals for the pageant were under way, and I was bound and determined to hang on to my coveted role as Mary. I was a little fatigued, and the nausea had mostly gone away, so I could participate, if only in a limited capacity. The rest of the cast was very understanding, and the director was willing to work around what I was able to do. Still, he insisted that I have an understudy just in case I was too ill on the night of the performance.

Fortunately, Mary traditionally wore a head scarf, and although a few wisps of hair were apparent on previous Marys, I don't think it was too noticeable. Still I was self-conscious.

Emily Masterson was playing Gabriel, and this particular evening at rehearsal when she made her entrance I couldn't help but notice her hair. Long and blonde and arranged in sausage curls that made her look more like a child than a mother of four. I just kept looking at it.

"Evelyn, Evelyn? Say your line," said the director from offstage. I had gotten so absorbed in Emily's hair that I had lost track of the dialogue, and so I blurted, "Why dost thou come hair?"

The whole cast froze. At first, I thought I was going to laugh, but instead big tears formed in my eyes and rolled down my cheeks. Emily, in spite of her fairly enormous wings, came over and gave me a hug and cried, too.

The crying was far from over, very far.

My last treatment was the day before the pageant. Tom and I walked into the waiting area and Sheila was standing there, which was odd. It was also obvious that something was wrong.

"Evelyn, Tom, I think you had better sit down," she said.

We sat down while whatever ominous news there was hung above us.

Sheila sat, too. She looked at me, and she looked at her hands, and then she looked back up at me.

"Evelyn, we got a call a little bit ago, and, well, there's no easy way to say this. . . ." Tears were forming in her eyes. "We just found out that," she paused a moment and took a deep breath, "we just found out that Lola died this morning."

Once again, like on the day I received my diagnosis, the room went into slow motion, and I wasn't seeing or hearing anything. Then, finally, I could hear, and what I heard was my sobbing, and I could see again, but my face was buried in Tom's chest with his arms around me. After several minutes, I managed to ask the question.

"How?"

"Well, chemo, as you know, is very hard on the body, and it looks like she had a heart attack. I'm so very sorry, Evelyn."

She told me that the doctor had said that if I wanted to skip my last treatment he thought it would be okay. So that's what I did.

I didn't say a word on the way home, and I went to the bedroom and crawled under the blankets and cried. Tom knew me well enough to know that I would want to be alone, but he came in every so often and gave me a kiss and told me he loved me.

It just wasn't fair. This wonderful, vivacious, joyful woman who looked death in the eye and winked was now gone. The cancer had won, and I had lost someone who had become a dear friend.

Tom made me eat something for dinner, but I told him I was too emotionally undone to go to rehearsal. He went over and told the cast what had happened and my understudy filled in for me.

The next day, I was no better. As the time for the performance drew near, I found Tom in the kitchen. I sat at the table with him.

"I don't think I can do it," I said.

"Do what?"

"The pageant."

"Oh, Evy, you know how important this is. You really should do it."

"It's so frivolous, Tom," I responded. "Lola's dead, and I go off to play Mary in an amateur pageant the next day. I think it would be disrespectful."

"You know that's not true, Evy," Tom said softly. "And you also know that Lola would want you to do it. She was ready to go home. She'd been ready for years, and she counted each day and every friend as a blessing and a cause for joy. She loved you. You'd be disrespecting her if you didn't do it."

I knew he was right, and so I reluctantly decided to go through with it.

Chemo lowers your immune system, so I was supposed to be careful about being around a lot of people. Consequently, I had my own room to get dressed in before the pageant, and someone was to come and get me.

At the appointed time, I was escorted to the dark stage. The opening scene was Mary sitting alone and had some lines about being young and poor but so in love with this man Joseph, and then Gabriel, Emily Masterson (the blonde), was to suddenly appear and deliver her lines.

I sat on the darkened stage waiting for the curtain to go up and stared at the floor. Here I was helping people to celebrate the most important event in history, and all I wanted to do was scream at God for taking Lola.

"Why do you do these things?" I whispered to God.

And then I heard Lola's voice in my head: "Sometimes you have to lose something before you realize how blessed you are."

The curtain went up, the spotlight hit me, I delivered my lines, and Emily entered from stage left. The other spotlight hit her and she began to deliver her lines.

She said, "I bring you great tidings of comfort and joy."

I had heard that line a hundred times, but it was very different tonight.

Comfort and joy. The words of my friend Lola came rushing back to me about how God was watching her, and how he would bring her home, and that this was going to happen to all of us eventually so every day we needed to count the blessings of our life, and that she ended with "Comfort and joy."

I looked into Emily's face, and then it hit me. Emily was bald. There wasn't a single strand of blonde hair on her head, let alone a sausage curl. I was stunned, but not so stunned that I didn't deliver my next lines.

Then four more angels made their entrance, and they were all bald, too. And every shepherd and every wise man, and, well, everyone in the cast was bald. They had all shaved their heads. Not one of them wore the part of the costume that was supposed to cover their heads.

The last scene of the pageant was of the entire cast gathered around the manger while everyone sang "Silent Night." I realized after the first verse that I was the only one with my head covered.

And so I slowly removed the scarf from my bald noggin. The audience burst into applause.

I looked out into the audience, and there my husband, Tom, sat in the front row, with his head shaved as well.

Later, I learned that the cast had talked about doing this for weeks, but when they learned of Lola's death, they decided that they needed to do it to honor her and to honor me. They had clued in the audience ahead of time. Everyone knew but me.

I realized then what I had to be thankful for. I also realized that my losses had allowed me to see the world differently. I saw it as a place that was temporary and knew that the sort of love that had been shown to me, both by my friends and God, would sustain me no matter what I had to go through.

Losses can be horrible. They wound and leave scars, but they can also be healing. I knew I didn't need to worry about Lola. She was in a better place. A place where there is no sorrow or pain. In that light, the loss of my hair seemed trivial, and my sadness over it was me being small.

The losses I experienced were painful, but God used them. God used them to show me how much I had to be grateful for. He used them as an opportunity for others to show their love for me in an exceptional way. He used them to bring me comfort and joy.

9

RENOVATIONS

If you had told me that getting mugged would change my life, I might have believed you, but if you had told me it would be the best thing that ever happened to me, I would have had my doubts.

From the time I was twelve, I've worked. My first job was selling papers at the mill gate after school, after the day shift. As a teen I worked weekends and summers for my uncle's construction company. I carried lumber, drove nails, poured concrete; anything that needed to be done I would do it. After high school I got a job at the mill and never missed a day's work. Didn't take any vacation either. When the mill closed, I mortgaged the house and started my own remodeling company. "Babe's Renovation," I called it. That's my name, Babe. Well, actually, my given name's Duane, but nobody but my mother ever called me that; everyone always called me Babe, since I was the youngest in the family. I still have never missed a day and I've never taken a nickel in an unemployment check.

I provide for myself. I don't need to be reliant on anyone else, and that's the way I want it. Complete independence.

I don't understand why people are always asking for handouts. There's no reason for it. If they just worked hard and applied themselves they could have everything they need. All of this talk about "helping those who don't have enough" is garbage. Nobody ever helped me . . . and I've done just fine.

I never married. I just never got around to it. I work twelve hours a day and then when I'm through I go and work on my own home. I've been building it for years now, although I'm not sure it will ever really be finished.

The Morgans had a problem with their bathroom. Actually, it was a problem that flooded the floor of the bathroom, soaked through the drywall of that room, ran under the floor, courtesy of a missing wax ring around the toilet, and flowed on down through the front hall chandelier onto the hardwood floor.

"Babe, am I glad to see you!" exclaimed Mrs. Morgan as I stepped through the door and into her little catastrophe.

I looked it over. "Reminds me of that Frank Lloyd Wright place," I quipped. "You know, Falling Water." She smiled faintly, too distraught over the damage to manage more.

"Babe, there are just ten days 'til Christmas and I'm supposed to be entertaining a crowd on Christmas Eve! Can you have this repaired by then?"

It so happened that the main job I was working on was being delayed while the owner and architect argued over the kitchen cabinets, so, with the exception of a few small jobs, I was free.

"Yeah, I think I can have it done by then," I said.

It's interesting working in someone's home the way I do. In some ways you become a part of the extended family. I had worked for the Morgans before, so it was even more pronounced this time. I'd arrive at 7:30 and Mrs. Morgan would hand me a cup of coffee. Mr. Morgan would be reading the paper at the kitchen table.

"G'morning, Mr. Morgan."

"Morning, Babe. How 'bout that game last night?"

"They'll never make it to the playoffs without better kicking."

I'd see their kids go off to school and be there when they got back. I'd hear the piano lessons, and try not to trip over the dog as

I carried drywall up the stairs. The Morgans seemed like a real nice family.

One day as I was sealing seams in the ceiling of the hallway, Mrs. Morgan came bustling through the door loaded down with armloads of packages.

"Let me help you, ma'am," I said, climbing down the ladder.

"Oh, Babe, thank you! I'll be right back," said Mrs. Morgan as she transferred the burden into my hands and then darted back out to her car for another heap.

She asked me to follow her to the dining room, where we laid everything out on the table. The bags were full of toys.

"Wow," I said. "Your kids are going to have one terrific Christmas."

Mrs. Morgan smiled. "These aren't for my children," she said. "These are for needy children."

"Oh." I said, in as uncritical a voice as I could muster.

Mrs. Morgan continued, "Several years ago my husband and I were overwhelmed by the amount of stuff under our tree. We have so much already we thought it was time to make a change. So . . . we decided that for our next Christmas we would give each of the children a couple of gifts and then we'd use the rest of the money to find ways to share with those who usually do without. Now after we open our presents we all go downtown and prepare and serve dinner to the homeless at one of the shelters. You know, the last few Christmases have been absolutely the best."

I must have had a funny look on my face. "Babe, what's wrong?" asked Mrs. Morgan.

"Well, I guess that's a real nice thing you all do," I said, "but if you just give stuff away like that, those people are never going to get any better. I don't understand why you would do this."

"Well, Christmas is a time of giving. I figure that since God gave his only Son to us, the least we can do is give to others. We're so grateful to God for his provision that it just feels right to share our abundance with others."

"But maybe they don't really deserve it."

"Deserve it? I'm sure that may be true, but none of us deserves the gift of God's Son. God didn't give Jesus to us because we were entitled to salvation but because he loved us. And I guess that's why we do this; as a response to God's amazing love for us."

"Well, not to be cynical, ma'am, but you don't know these people. They could sell this nice stuff for drugs."

"Babe," said Mrs. Morgan, "most of these people are folks that have fallen on hard times. That could happen to any of us."

"Nah, it could never happen to me, Mrs. Morgan." I shook my head, and went back to work.

It was a complete mystery to me why these people would give away perfectly good stuff to people they had never even met. Mr. Morgan worked hard for what he had. It didn't seem right that he would give stuff to parasites lazing around, expecting handouts. And this stuff about God . . . what kind of foolishness is that? Giving his son at Christmas; what a lot of nonsense.

Later that afternoon I had to go into town to get some plumbing supplies. I arrived to find on the door of the shop a hand-scribbled note that read, "Be back in 10 minutes." So I waited out in front of the store. It was cold and gray, and snow was beginning to fall. I shoved my hands into my pockets.

"Excuse me, sir."

The voice came from behind me and I turned to see a most unusual group of men. One was gangly and wore a threadbare overcoat. The second, short and squat, was arrayed in an army coat and a bright pink knit winter cap. The third fellow, who was speaking, wore an old trench coat; he was missing an arm.

"I'm wondering if you could spare some change for us." He was very polite and well spoken, and in spite of being outnumbered, I really didn't feel threatened.

"No," I said firmly.

"Bad man," said the guy in the pink hat, looking at the ground.

"Please, sir, it's Christmas," said the guy in the trench coat.

"What? Give you guys money so you can spend it on booze or God knows what else? I don't think so."

"Small heart," said Pink Hat.

"We just need to buy some food," said Trench Coat.

"Get lost," I said firmly. "You're not getting any handouts from me."

"Frozen soul," muttered Pink Hat.

Trench Coat nodded at me, oddly enough, with a look of pity. "Well, God bless you," he said in a tone that conveyed nothing but sincerity and they were off down the street.

The store opened and I went in for my supplies.

B & W Hardware is one of those old-time stores that you just don't find many of anymore. Stuff hangs from the ceiling and every corner seems to have some odd or end. I don't even look for things there; I just tell Wilma what I need. (Wilma's the "W" in B & W; her husband, Bob, died years ago.) She's tough as nails, a rail thin old lady who's seen a lot in her seventy-plus years. She could remember when the store first opened and this part of the city was a bustling commerce center. Now most of the stores had closed and I often wondered how much longer she could hold out.

As she gathered onto the old wooden counter the supplies I needed, I told her the story of what had happened outside the store.

"Oh, I know those guys," she said. "They don't mean any harm."

"I just resent being asked to give handouts to people who don't do anything to improve themselves."

"You know, Babe, we shouldn't take God's blessings for granted."

"Oh, please, Wilma, what's God ever done for me? Everything I have I've earned."

"Oh, really? Like your health, and your considerable talents as a builder, and your family, who instilled such a good work ethic in you. Did you earn those?"

I'd known Wilma all my life, and she was an old lady. It didn't seem right to lose my temper with her, so out of respect for her I didn't say anything.

Wilma looked up from the counter. "And besides, Babe, you never know when you're going to meet Jesus."

"I'm not dying anytime soon."

"That's not what I mean, Babe. Jesus said, 'When you do unto the least of these, you do unto me.'"

"Aw, Wilma, spare me the religion lesson."

"Well, Babe, you'll listen if you know what's good for you," she said, filling a box with the supplies. "Remember, Jesus was born homeless."

"Well, things are different now," I said.

"Don't be so quick to judge people, Babe. You don't know their story. Sometimes things happen that we can't control. Things can happen to any of us."

"I don't think so, Wilma." I turned and left.

As I finished up the project at the Morgans' place, these conversations played in my mind. Mrs. Morgan saying it's good to give to others because God loved us, Wilma telling me that I never knew when I was going to meet Jesus, that strange little pink-hatted guy calling me a bad man, and the phrase, "Things can happen to any of us." I knew this wasn't true, but it kept echoing in my head like some kind of unearthly warning.

Christmas Eve arrived and I was putting the final touches of paint on the ceiling moldings in the hallway as Mrs. Morgan prepared for her guests. The party would start at 7:00 and afterward everyone would head to church together. Didn't sound like much of a party to me, but, hey, to each his own.

Mrs. Morgan came into the hallway to survey the finished work. "Babe, I don't know how to thank you enough," she said.

"No thanks necessary," I responded. "It's just what I do."

"May I ask what you're doing for Christmas?"

Actually, I wasn't doing anything special. I'd probably spend the day working on some of the trim work at my house.

"Oh, nothing much," I said.

"Well, we'd love it if you'd come with us to the shelter to serve dinner."

You've got to be kidding, I thought to myself. *Give up practically the only day I have off to feed a bunch of deadbeats? I don't think so. You won't find me in some pathetic shelter on Christmas.* I smiled and managed to say, "That's very nice of you, Mrs. Morgan, but I think I'll just take the day to myself."

The project was done, and there were a few items I hadn't needed so I drove down to Wilma's to return them. It was snowing heavily and the radio was extending severe winter storm warnings for the area. I parked in an alley next to the store and pulled the box of items from the back of the truck. But when I got to the store, the door was locked. A sign read, "Merry Christmas! Will reopen Dec. 26."

I returned to the alley with the box.

"Hey, mister," a voice sneered from a doorway. I ignored it but my heart began to race. I placed the box in the truck.

"I'm talking to you," said the voice, and out of the corner of my eye I caught a glimpse of a huge man in a black coat stepping into the alley with a baseball bat. "Merry Christmas," he said, rushing at me, and then everything went black.

When I woke up, I found myself lying on the floor of a dimly lit room. My head was spinning and throbbing hard. I tried to get up but found that I was too weak.

"Whoa, mister, you just lie still there; you've had a nasty blow to your head."

I tried to focus my eyes and eventually accomplished this. "Where am I?"

"Well, you're with us, in our home. We found you lying in an alley covered with snow. It's a wonder you're not dead."

And then another voice said, "Bad man."

I knew that voice. Squinting through the dim light I could see a ratty old couch near me, and sitting on it was a demented-looking man in a pink knit cap. A little drool was escaping from the corner of his mouth.

The first voice said, "What's your name?"

"Babe." But it wasn't me who responded; it was the guy on the couch in the pink cap.

My head was clearing now. "How . . . how did he know that?" I managed.

"Oh, that's Clifford; he's what you call a clairvoyant. I don't understand how he knows stuff, but he does."

Now I could see who was talking. It was a guy in an old flannel shirt with the left sleeve pinned to the shoulder. He only had one arm. "Here, drink this," he offered, kneeling down to hand me an old coffee cup with something warm in it.

I took a sip. "What is this?"

"Coffee," said the one-armed man, "with a little kick in it. Thought you might need it, considering what you've been through." Then he added, "I'm Jesus."

This was going from bad to worse.

"What happened to me?"

"Near as I can tell you were mugged."

"Baseball bat," said Clifford, shaking his head.

I managed to sit up. I felt my pockets: no wallet, no keys, no money. I rubbed my forehead. "How do I know you didn't take my stuff?"

"Oh, that makes sense," said Jesus, in a tone implying I was an idiot. "The savior of the world takes your stuff and then takes you to his home to lie about it."

Right now very little was making sense. "Sorry," I said. "I didn't mean anything by it."

"Yes, you did," said Clifford, looking randomly at the ceiling. Then he giggled.

"Well, Babe, looks like you're going to be with us for a while."

"No!" I said. "I need to call someone to come get me or call the police."

"We don't have a phone. And it's snowing so heavily that they've closed most of the roads into the city. You just sit tight."

This couldn't be happening. I looked around the room and discovered that what they were calling "home" was just one room.

A couch, a cot, a table, a couple of chairs, a sink, and a small fridge. "Where am I?"

"This is our home," said Jesus. "It's not much, bathroom's down the hall, but it beats lying in an alley during a snowstorm."

"And who are you guys?"

"Well, as I said before, I'm Jesus and that's Clifford and over there is George." Seated in the corner was a tall, balding man who stared off into space as if I weren't there.

"You guys brothers?"

"Heavens, no," said Jesus, standing over a hot plate on the table, dishing something into a bowl. "I don't know much about these guys really. Here, eat this." He nodded, handing me a bowl of hot chicken noodle soup. I dug in; I swear it was the best chicken noodle soup I'd ever tasted.

"Clifford, get up now," directed Jesus. Clifford rose from the couch. "Babe, go lie down there," said Jesus, and I followed his instructions. He pulled a chair up near the couch for himself and another for Clifford.

"I was wounded in the Army," said Jesus, pointing to the missing arm. "I get some benefits, but no one wants Jesus working for them so I have this place and manage to get by. These two," he explained, pointing at Clifford, now gnawing on an unpeeled banana, and at George, who was still sitting motionless in the corner, "I met wandering the streets. I'm not sure Clifford is right in the head." Then Jesus added sotto voce, taking the banana away from Clifford and peeling it for him, "But he has this bizarre knack for knowing stuff. Watch this: Hey, Clifford, when will the snow stop?"

"Fifty-two minutes," said Clifford through a mouthful of banana.

"Ain't that something?!" marveled Jesus.

"Well," I began, and looked at my watch, which wasn't there.

Jesus looked at a clock on the wall. "Well, we'll see. He said fifty-two minutes, which will be exactly midnight." Then he motioned to George. "Near as I can tell he's a deaf mute. Hasn't said a word in two years."

We sat in silence for a long time.

"Why do these guys live with you?" I asked.

"Because they have nowhere else to go. I have so much, it just seemed like the right thing to do to give them a place to stay."

To say this was the most bizarre night of my life would be an understatement—mugged in an alley on Christmas Eve and waking up in a meager one-room apartment with a deaf mute, a clairvoyant in a pink hat, and a delusional guy who thinks he's Jesus.

But what else was going on here? Mrs. Morgan had said that she was able to give because God loved her, and Wilma had scolded me for being so selfish. And here was this one-armed crazy man who had practically nothing and he'd taken in two homeless people. Delusional and poor, yes, but I realized he was more of a human being than I was.

And then it occurred to me that maybe this wasn't all an accident, that maybe God did have his hand in this. It was just too bizarre to have happened any other way. And that maybe this was God's way of showing me in some infinitely strange way that he loved me, too.

And then from some seldom-visited recess of my cold and stubborn heart, a place that I hadn't visited in years, came my next words. . . .

"Thank you, Jesus, you saved my life."

"You're welcome," he replied. "Want some more soup?"

Clifford said, "We've had a breakthrough."

"Look!" said Jesus, walking to the only window. "It's stopped snowing and it's midnight. Clifford, you are really something."

Then I fell asleep.

I woke the next morning to find standing over me my three new friends. Each was dressed a little nicer. While the clothes still looked like battered hand-me-downs, George and Clifford were wearing neckties over their sweatshirts, and Jesus had managed to find an old plaid sports coat with huge lapels, complemented with a loudly striped tie.

"Boy, you slept real good," said Jesus.

"He's better now," said Clifford.

George just stared vacantly into my face.

"It's time for dinner," said Jesus.

"Great," I said, "I'm starving. What are we having?"

"I don't know," said Jesus. "We're going out."

"Going out for dinner?"

"Turkey," said Clifford.

"He's uncanny, isn't he?" remarked Jesus.

I got up from the couch. There was only a faint remnant of my headache from the night before. I was sore all over, though, either from the mugging or the couch, I still don't know. Jesus handed me an old overcoat. "Here, better wear this," he said. "It's cold outside." I did so and we went out on the street.

As Clifford had predicted, the snow had stopped the night before, giving road crews plenty of time to clear things up. Huge piles of snow lined the street and the bright sun reflecting off of it made us all squint until we were almost blind.

Jesus headed down the street at a brisk pace, with Clifford and George following close behind. I observed this curious group leading me and wondered what was going to happen to them, as I would surely find my way home by tonight. And I was surprised to find myself content for now to be with this trio.

We walked for several blocks until we came to a large redbrick church. The Church of the Nativity, proclaimed a sign. Somehow I wasn't surprised. Jesus had obviously been here before. He walked through the front doors and then immediately turned down a set of steps to the basement. Passing through a set of double doors we entered into a huge room filled with tables and lots of people eating. At the far end was a serving line. The aroma was heavenly.

Jesus picked up a tray and handed it to me. "You go first."

Someone placed a salad on my tray and then some Jell-O with little marshmallows on it (I love that), someone else added a plate with mashed potatoes, and then someone slung some green beans on that. Next was the entrée, which, as Clifford had accurately predicted, was turkey. A woman asked whether I wanted white meat or dark, and then she said, "Babe?"

I realized then that I hadn't looked any of these people in the eye; now I met the gaze of Mrs. Morgan. "Babe, my heavens, what happened to you? Are you all right?" Not waiting for a response, she rushed around the end of the serving line, took me by the shoulder, and looked me in the face. "Your eyes are black and blue; you have a gash on your forehead. Where did you get this coat?" And then she gave me a tremendous hug.

The next thing I knew Mr. Morgan had his big arms around us, and the kids were joining in. I began to cry.

And then, looking up again, I realized that the whole place had come to a standstill and everyone was looking at us. I began to laugh, loud and deep. I looked at the Morgans and said simply, "I'm fine now. I met Jesus."

I turned to my new friends. Standing with them was Wilma with a tray full of dirty dishes. She smiled wryly and said, "I told you you'd never know when you were going to meet Jesus."

Indeed I had met Jesus, but what I would come to realize is that I had met him numerous times before. I'd met him in the Morgan family, who loved those they didn't know more than they loved what the world offered. I'd met him in an old lady who cared enough about me to tell me I was wrong, and then I met him in a disabled vet who, while not *the* Jesus, was, even in the midst of madness, more Christlike than anyone else I had ever met.

While the guy who mugged me with the baseball bat certainly didn't intend to, he'd actually knocked some sense into me. More importantly, he knocked some faith into me. The mugging allowed me to see that those I thought of as weak were actually strong and that those who are generous are the richest folks in the world, whether they have much or little to begin with. He allowed me to see finally a God who is bigger than I am, and to get to know Jesus, whose birth allows me to love those around me. Being mugged ended up being the best thing that ever happened to me, because through it I came to know Jesus.

10

THE GIFT GIVER

I'm an office manager. I know it's not the sort of profession one aspires to, but for a young woman such as myself, who never finished school, it fits the bill. I make sure that the partners in this law firm are in the right place at the right time. I see that the secretarial staff is doing its job. I make sure that everything flows the right way. I'm very good at it.

The one part of my job I hate, though, is buying Christmas gifts for everyone. Years ago, when the firm was smaller, we fended for ourselves, but when that got too expensive for us, we went another direction.

One of the secretaries got the idea actually. She was on a tear because of the foul language around the office, so she started a "cuss fund." Every time someone used profanity he or she had to put a quarter in the jar. At first we thought it would be a good way to clean up everyone's act, but some of the people around here actually took pride in the amount they had contributed. At the end of the first year we had over a thousand dollars lying around, and it was decided that the money would be used to buy everyone in the office one gift. Pretty ironic.

The task fell to me. Actually, it should have posed no problem, considering the skills I possess. But there was something daunting about the whole idea. I mean, you work with people every day and yet you really don't know them—what it is they like or don't like, what they might want or what they might throw away.

The first year I bought everybody tickets to a show that was coming to town. That was fine but not very personal. The second year I gave everyone gift certificates to a fancy restaurant, a nice gesture but lacking that certain flair. This year I was determined to buy each person something unique, something that would really speak to him or her. I started to look for information early with the idea that by finding out something about each person I could get that special gift. Three days before Christmas I still hadn't bought a single item.

That's why I stayed late at the office by myself that evening, poring over catalogues, desperate for inspiration. *Maybe I'll just buy everyone hockey tickets or a nice bottle of something*, I thought. "God, I need a miracle," I muttered.

That's when I looked up from the catalogue and saw a man standing in the room. I jumped and gasped.

"I'm sorry, Myra, I didn't mean to startle you." He smiled.

He was an older man, probably retired, and he was nicely dressed in a dark suit. He sported a thick, close-cropped head of gray hair, and he stood very erect. He had these blue-gray eyes that reminded me of the ocean. Oddly, I didn't feel particularly afraid.

"Ah . . . who are . . . um . . . you know my name?"

"Yes, I do," was his kindly reply.

"Well, ah, who are you? What are you doing here?"

"I'm the answer to your prayer."

"Prayer? What prayer?"

"I've come to help with the gifts."

My mouth just hung open. I had heard about a service in town that helped people select gifts and even sent someone out to make the purchases. I had in fact called them that afternoon, but they said I was too late, too close to Christmas Day. Maybe this man was from that agency.

"Somebody sent you?"

"Oh, most definitely."

"And you're going to help me buy these gifts?"

"Actually, no. I'm going to take care of all of it."

"All of it?"

"Yes."

"How can you do that? I mean, it's three days before Christmas and the stores are a mess; and you don't even know the people here. I want *personal* gifts. How are you going to do that without knowing these people?"

"Oh, I know a lot more than you might think." He smiled confidently.

I was in a very tight spot. "You can really do this?"

"Yes, I can. You leave everything to me. I understand the Christmas party is the twenty-fourth. I'll have everything ready." He made a very gentlemanly bow and walked briskly out of the room.

I sat there for a moment, stunned, then ran after him. He was nowhere to be seen. The really strange thing was that the double glass doors into the hallway were still locked.

I wasn't sure whether to feel relieved or more nervous, but given the late date I had no other choice but to trust this stranger.

The twenty-fourth came quickly and, as you might expect, not much work was getting done. After lunch people started to set up for the Christmas party and by four it was in full swing. There was more merriment in the office for this brief time than we saw all year. Maybe it was the drinking or maybe just the holiday spirit, but people really let their hair down.

"Hey, Myra. Where are those gifts?" yelled someone above the very loud music. "What is it this year, hockey tickets?" People laughed. I cringed. There *were* no gifts, not yet.

"Maybe it's a good bottle of hooch," someone else offered rhetorically.

"Yeah, well, with your mouth you should get two!" another shouted back. There was more laughter.

Now it was after five and still there were no gifts. Maybe I'd been dreaming. Maybe that man had never been there in my office. This was going to be a disaster. I could feel it. I slipped away to my office and closed the door. I sat there in the dark looking at the city lights.

What I didn't know was that as soon as I left, a delivery man showed up with a whole cart full of individually wrapped gifts.

I sat there in the darkness about to cry.

Something was wrong. I listened for a minute. That was it; it was *quiet*. What moments ago had been a wild cacophony of celebration was now more silent than a normal workday. Now I was really worried. What was going on? What could have made the party stop? One thing was certain—I was not going back out there to learn the answer. I sat for a couple of minutes waiting for something to happen.

It did.

There was a quiet knock on my door.

I realize it sounds silly now, but I didn't know what to do. I sat still for a minute, and then it came again. I turned on the desk lamp and managed to say in my most authoritative voice, "Come in."

It was Ryan. He was our hot-shot family practice lawyer. That means divorce. Young and ambitious, he had the reputation for being a real shark. But I had never seen him like this. He seemed totally at peace. He was carrying a small box.

"I um . . . I . . . ah, just wanted to say thank you."

"You're welcome," I replied. "For what?"

He laid the box on my desk. Inside I could see two small gray mittens both for the same hand.

"How did you do this?" he asked.

"Um, just a lucky guess," I offered, very confused.

He was silent a moment. "My mother died when I was ten. Cancer. The winter before she died, when we knew she was very sick, she decided that she would knit me a pair of mittens. We even went to the store and picked out the color. I remember telling her I wanted gray because then no one would know when they were dirty." He smiled. "She had never knit anything before and she worked on them for what seemed like weeks. When they were finally finished she made a big deal out of giving them to me and then discovered to her shock and my horror that she had knit two right hands. I remember being upset. Not because she had gotten it wrong but because I felt bad for her. She so wanted me to have these. But what I remember now is how she laughed, a very deep uninhibited laugh, and how she swept me into her arms and held me very close. She told me not to worry, that everything would be okay. And you know, I felt a lot better." There was a tear running down his face. "Thanks, Myra, you gave me back my mom."

He left the room silently. To say I was stunned would have been an understatement.

About a minute later Rachel appeared. Rachel was considered the office tramp. She was wildly single and was rumored to have slept with most of the partners. Consequently, she wasn't very well liked by most people. She stood in the doorway a moment.

"Where did you get these?" she asked, walking over and placing a box on my desk that contained two well-worn ballet slippers. Each was clearly marked "Rachel."

I had no reply.

"When I was eight," she began, "I had this dream to be a dancer. I watched a ballet on TV and thought that it was the most beautiful thing I had ever seen. I told my parents that I wanted ballet lessons but they laughed. I was too clumsy; it would be a waste of money. But then my uncle Mort found out. He was sort of the black sheep of the family and my parents didn't like him very much. But one day he dropped by the house and gave me this box with ballet slippers in it and said he had it all arranged. Every Saturday for years he picked me up at 9:00 and I went off to Madame Ricardo's ballet school. You know, I wasn't very good and I didn't get much more graceful, but what a feeling to know that someone believed in me and cared about me. Tonight I remembered . . ." her voice broke, ". . . I remembered what it felt like to be loved." She smiled. "Thanks, Myra," she said. She picked up the box and left the room.

For the next two hours the same sort of thing happened to me over and over again. I saw a tennis racquet, a trombone, several party dresses, a corsage, a set of dog tags, a lace handkerchief, some ticket stubs, a five-dollar gold piece, a stuffed lion, a cereal bowl, a baseball glove, and even a real live golden retriever, to name a few. Everyone came with a story about something forgotten but now remembered, something lost and now found.

The offices were quiet again because everyone had left for the holiday. But when I looked at the door again there was a familiar figure.

"It's you!" I exclaimed.

The stranger who had met me several nights ago was there.

"Myra, there was one gift left."

He walked over and placed a small, brightly wrapped box on my desk. I looked at it for a moment.

"It's for you," he said.

I hesitated but finally opened it. There, nestled in cotton, was a small porcelain Jesus lying in a manger. I gasped. It looked just like . . . but it couldn't be. I picked it up, turned it over, and there on the bottom were the words *MAD IN FRANCE.*

I simply stared.

"You recognize it?"

"Yes," I said. "My aunt Edith brought this back with her from a trip to Europe. It was part of an entire nativity scene she gave to my parents. We used to kid her because it said 'mad in France' on the bottom. Uncle Edwin said it was characteristic of their whole trip." I stopped and laughed quietly. "But how . . . I mean it was . . . I . . ."

"Yes?"

I took a deep breath. "I was seventeen and I wanted to go to the West Coast with this boy I was crazy about, Ben . . . Ben was his name. I was going to drop out of school and we were going to leave on his bike. That was pretty common back then."

The man stood silently listening.

"It was a few days before Christmas when I told my parents my plans. They forbade me to go, of course, wanted me to stay in school. It got pretty ugly. I yelled and they yelled. They said I was ruining my life and that I didn't know what I was doing. That I would be sorry if I followed through. I got hysterical and I . . . I picked up this little manger from the nativity set and I threw it at my father." I paused, remembering the pain.

"And?" said the stranger.

"It missed him and hit the wall behind him, shattering into a thousand pieces." I paused again. I could see the hurt on my parents' faces, the horror that things had gotten so out of control. I could see the grief in my father's eyes.

"I left that night," I continued. "I never really did come home. But, you know, the funny thing was that all the while I was out there my parents never gave up on me. They wrote and called and encouraged me and when Ben left me for someone else they asked me to come home. But I was too embarrassed. I just . . . I just couldn't.

"When I finally did manage enough courage to visit one Christmas, there was the manger scene out on the coffee table with the baby missing. It was very hard to look at. My father noticed me staring at it. He came over and put his arms around me and told me not to worry, that we all did things that we regretted but that it was all right. He said . . ." I was fighting back tears.

"Yes . . . go on."

"He said he loved me and nothing could ever change that." I began to cry. "You know, now that I see this, I understand something."

"What is that?" asked the stranger.

I gazed down at the tiny porcelain baby. "Forgiveness."

I looked up and he was gone. I searched the entire office and he couldn't be found.

There is a church across the street from the office. "All Angels," they call it. I put my coat on and hurried over, slipping inside during the evening service. I had never been there before, hadn't been inside a church in years, but it brought back a flood of memories. The smell of burning candles, the dim, negative-looking images of stained glass at night, the mystery of being in God's presence. I sat down in a pew and listened to the familiar carols and the even more familiar story about the birth of a baby. My eyes strayed to the stained glass window behind the altar. It showed the angels greeting the shepherds on a cold December night. I stared hard at it. That angel in the center, he looked familiar. Where had I seen him before? Suddenly it dawned on me. That was the face of the stranger. I gasped audibly, and several people turned around to see if I was all right. I assured them, very truthfully, that I was.

The next day when I visited my parents, I slipped the tiny porcelain figure in its manger back into the crèche. Somehow the whole thing made sense. I knew that the scene I was staring at had been made complete. Something that had been broken was now whole and it was as much me as it was the tiny figure. For the first time I understood what it meant to be cared for by a Father who never gave up on me.

I found my father standing in the kitchen. I threw my arms around him and wished him a merry Christmas. My eyes welled with tears and I said, "Dad, thank you for the gift of love."

My parents never asked about Jesus's reappearance. It was as if they just understood.

11

WE THREE KINGS

It was snowing, and it was snowing hard. Large featherlike flakes drifted down in the calm night air, some landing on the windshield, others swirling or whisked over the windshield, falling on the road behind me. The wipers beat back and forth, a steady rhythm to an unsung song.

Most people dream of a white Christmas, but this was becoming a nightmare. It had been snowing like this all day long, and the drifts were now several feet deep in places, and the roads, though plowed earlier, were slick and covered again. To make matters worse, I was unfamiliar with this country road, which twisted and turned into the unending darkness always just ahead, with nothing but woods on either side. It had been half an hour since I'd passed another car and longer still since I'd seen a house. I couldn't be certain I hadn't taken a wrong turn.

"Let's do Christmas in the country this year!" my wife had suggested cheerily one warm autumn day. I was barely paying attention, and Christmas seemed so far away that I nodded absently.

"Arthur," she said in a slightly scolding tone. "Are you listening to me?"

I looked up from the financial page. "Of course I'm listening," I replied.

"All right, then. What did I say?"

"You were talking about how they celebrate Christmas in another country."

"Honestly, Arthur," she fumed. "I said no such thing. I said, 'Let's celebrate Christmas in the country.'"

"Patrice, we live in Manhattan."

"I am fully cognizant of that fact! That's precisely why I want to go to the country. We'll take the girls and rent a house in Vermont; it will be a lovely change, won't it, Arthur?"

"Yes," I lied.

Patrice had been reading an article about winter getaways in the Sunday travel section; she decided then and there that we would be taking our two girls to spend Christmas in an idyllic setting of bucolic bliss.

I went back to the financial section.

I'd been making a lot of money for the past several years. I used to work for a brokerage firm, but after making a bundle through tech stocks and IPOs, I quit to take on the management of my own money. It's a full-time job, and I've done very well with it—so well, in fact, that my family has no worries at all. The girls attend the finest schools; we have an enormous, impeccably furnished apartment on the Upper East Side; and our social life is brisk and full. I'm rich now, rich as a king—a rather amusing phrase in this case, as my surname is King. Being king is good, I find; very good, indeed.

However, with my efforts focused on managing the wealth, I can't be spending much energy around the apartment attending to the minutiae of daily life, so I acquiesced to Patrice's dream, and she finalized plans for the family to spend Christmas in Vermont.

Now I was worried, as the back of the car skidded occasionally on the slick road somewhere in rural Vermont, and the snow beat down harder and faster.

Several weeks before Christmas I'd been enjoying lunch with Bob Hunter, an old college friend. He runs a foundation in the city that supports a variety of charitable organizations.

"The market's wild right now, isn't it?" he said as the soup was served.

"Not wild," I replied. "Just very, very good."

"A lot of people are making a lot of money."

"Yes, sirree," I acknowledged, letting him know I was among them. "Must be pretty good for you too," I added.

He was quiet for a while, in deep contemplation of the soup cooling on his spoon. "Arthur," he started finally. "Arthur, do you ever give anything away?"

I nearly choked. "I should say not!" I said sharply. "I have no desire to support the riffraff."

Bob eyed me uneasily. "You know, Arthur, we've known each other for a long time now, and, well . . . I'm a bit concerned about you."

"Concerned about me?!"

"Well, yes. I watch as you acquire more and more wealth, but it never seems to be enough. You never seem satisfied, and to my knowledge you never give anything back."

"And that has you worried?"

"Yes, of course."

"Why would you be concerned about such a thing? Are the foundation's coffers running low?"

"Arthur, I'll ignore that comment. I'm concerned because . . . it's just not good for you."

"Not good for me? It's tremendous for me! I've amassed enough to protect myself to eternity. I have more than I could ever have imagined back in our undergrad days."

"That's the point," Bob replied. "You have more than you could ever imagine, yet it's not enough. You're driven to want more and more for yourself. Doesn't that worry you?"

"No. You worry me."

There was awkward silence for a moment. I felt a little bad at having been so brusque with him. "Why," I asked, "is this so important to you?"

"I just think that we're blessed with so much . . . rather, that God blesses us with so much that we should give back. You know, money is not what matters most."

Great, I thought, *just what I need—a religion lesson.*

"God?" I exclaimed. "What in the world has God got to do with this?"

"It's a matter of recognizing that we are dependent on something greater than ourselves."

"I'm dependent on no one, and I'll be doggoned if anyone will be dependent on me!"

"Arthur," he said softly. "Patrice and the girls are dependent on you, to begin with; and secondly . . ." He trailed off.

I looked at him over my plate questioningly. "And secondly?"

". . . and secondly, you need to be careful lest you become possessed by your possessions. You should be giving something back to God."

I was incredulous. *How dare you preach at me*, I thought, but our long friendship kept me from voicing my indignation.

Regretfully, Bob was not finished with his discourse. "Arthur, a man who only 'takes' has a very small life; you need to give something back, if only for your own good. You need to get your priorities straight."

To keep from losing my temper, I changed the subject to basketball and, thankfully, the matter was dropped.

Still, his words kept coming back to me. Had I become selfish and ungiving? Was I possessed by my possessions? The questions kept surfacing in my mind, but I kept pushing them away.

The snow was getting worse and the night seemed to be getting darker. I had a bad feeling about this.

A week earlier, Patrice had been packing for the trip. "Maybe we'll run into Bing Crosby and Danny Kaye," she said dreamily.

"Who are they?" asked Clara, my eight-year-old.

"They're dead," I said.

"Why would we want to see dead people in Vermont?"

"I don't know. Ask your mother."

"Oh, honestly," moaned Patrice. "Must you put a damper on everything, Arthur?" She didn't waste a moment buying the movie *White Christmas* so the girls would know what she was talking about.

I'm not all that big on Christmas, with its excessive emphasis on random giving. I have no problem giving gifts to family and friends, but it seems that everyone has their hand out at this time of year. You can hardly enter a store on Fifth Avenue without running into one of those blasted bell ringers. "Give to the poor." I say, let the poor just get jobs.

At any rate, I go along with Christmas because it's expected. Tradition. That's the only reason.

Patrice had rented a house for two weeks, so she went up early with the girls. I was to drive up the day before Christmas and arrive in time to go to church, of all things. I wouldn't be away too long, though, as I had my investments to watch.

That's how I came to be driving on an unfamiliar country road in a heavy snow on Christmas Eve. Another man would have found it beautiful, I suppose. I found it annoying.

Then, abruptly, the car stopped. It didn't chug or gurgle or backfire or make any noise at all. It just stopped cold, and I drifted into the snow at the side of the road. I tried to start it up but there was no noise from the engine at all. I got out and opened the hood. I looked at the engine, which may as well have been a nuclear reactor for all I knew about auto mechanics. I slammed the hood loudly. I was white-hot with anger.

I didn't know exactly where I was, and the snow was only getting deeper. I knew for certain I was ruining my new calfskin loafers. Desolate, colder out than I'd imagined, everything blanketed in snow, this was a truly silent night. But not the stuff of sentimental Christmas carols. It never occurred to me until later that I might well have died from exposure.

There had to be something I could do. I would figure a way out of this. But nothing came to me. I popped open the hood once again, hoping for some miraculous insight, and just stood in the snow staring at the engine. After a time, I rested my forehead on my gloved hand on the propped hood, as if maybe some sort of inspiration would emanate from the expired engine.

"Whatcha *doin'* out here on a night like this?"

I physically left the ground. Out of the utter silence had burst a clearly audible, cackling question. I reeled around, landing back on my feet, to find before me the oddest creature.

"Boy, you scare real good," she laughed. "Wish I'da had myself one of those camera things, you know, with the film that pops out after a minute—even you'd find it funny."

It was a woman, not some ghostly figment of my imagination, but certainly unlike any woman I had ever come across. Actually, as I recall the incident, she resembled the homeless people who sleep on the benches near the river, only a little crazier.

She was rail thin and wearing a huge heavy wool coat likely obtained at an army surplus store. Her feet were shod in a pair of men's work boots with bright pink laces and she wore an ancient leather aviator's cap, its goggles resting on her forehead. Around her neck was a turquoise scarf that hung nearly to her knees.

"Got a name?" She squinted at me with one eye as though I might disappear at any moment.

"Ah, why, yes," I stammered, trying to assess the situation. "King. Arthur King."

"Whoa!" she whooped. "Pull the sword from the stone; we got us another king!" She slapped her hands together, which made no noise, being covered with fingerless rag wool gloves.

"No," I said in protest. "I'm no king; that's just my name."

She eyed me suspiciously. "King Kong, corn king, king size, super king size." She spun around in a circle, reciting the phrases like a little rhyme. Fastened to the back of her coat was a fluorescent orange triangle, the kind they put on slow-moving machinery.

"King cobra, King James English, King Coal, Nat King Cole . . ."

"Enough!" I shouted.

She halted abruptly, and her eyes narrowed in on me. I thought she might pounce like some distempered cat, but her face softened, and she said, "Bet you're cold."

Indeed I was. "Well," I said, "I think I'll just get back in my car."

"Makes no difference to me whether you freeze inside or outside the blasted thing. By the way, they've closed the road forty miles behind you and on ahead practically to Majestic."

"Majestic?"

"Next town, on up the road maybe five miles. I'll take you there."

"You've got a car?"

"Nope. I got a camel."

"A camel?"

"Yep."

"I'll wait here."

"Suit yourself," and she started off into the woods. And then she added, "Careful of the wolves."

She disappeared into the trees, singing merrily, "Kingfisher, King Charles spaniel, Burger King . . ."

I got back in the car and sat there. Now what was I going to do? The cell phone had no service and it was nearly as cold in the car by this time as it was outside. "She's right," I thought aloud. "I'm going to freeze to death here. Maybe I should have gone with her."

Then I heard a sound like a chainsaw or a big lawn mower, and I saw a light coming right at me from the woods. The sound grew steadily and the light enlarged as if I were stuck on train tracks facing an oncoming locomotive. Instinctively I ducked down onto the seat. The sound roared ever louder and the light grew more glaring and shifted direction; then abruptly there was silence. I raised my eyes to the window. Perched on a snowmobile towing a sled was the same crazy woman. Goggles now covering her eyes, she smiled broadly and waved dramatically. Painted on the side of the machine in beautifully stenciled letters were the words *Sopwith Camel*.

I have nothing to lose, I thought, and got out of the car.

"You'll still take me to Majestic?" I asked.

"The king's changed his mind, then?" She chortled as if she had won some important argument.

"I'd appreciate it. I'll give you something for your trouble."

"Arty, I doubt you've ever given anything to anyone," she scoffed.

"I've got cash." I was feeling a little desperate now. "A lot of cash."

She wrinkled her nose. "Pah! Worthless paper. What else you got?"

"What do you want? I can get you practically anything."

"How 'bout a perfume bottle? I collect 'em."

Joy of joys! Among the Christmas gifts in the car was a bottle of expensive perfume I had bought for Patrice.

"This is your lucky night," I said, retrieving the bottle from the car. I presented it to her, adding, "It's called *Beaucoup de Rien*. Very expensive."

She took the bottle out of the box, opened it, and sniffed.

"Whoa, Arthur, I think this stuff's gone bad!" She whistled, went "Phew," and without a thought turned the bottle upside down and sprinkled several hundred dollars' worth of French perfume into the snow. "Nice bottle, though," she declared, thrusting it deep into her coat pocket. "Hop on."

I did, and she started the engine.

"Wait," I shouted. "I never asked your name."

"Oh," she said. "I'm Sky King." She revved the engine and we took off into the night at a blinding speed.

We moved surprisingly fast over the drifts of snow. The night air stung my face. After two or three miles, she slowed down considerably and slipped the snowmobile down a path.

"Is this the way to Majestic?" I asked.

"Nope. Gotta make a stop first."

"What for?"

"Gotta get us another King."

Maybe accepting this woman's offer of help had been a mistake after all.

We wound down the single-lane road and eventually saw a glow of lights emanating from a modest wood frame house nestled in the woods.

We stopped in front of the house and Sky King turned off her Sopwith Camel. She turned in her seat and said, "Now, this is the Regals' place. They don't have much. I want you to mind your manners."

Insulted by this remark, I nonetheless determined to remain calm. "Why are we here?"

"Pickup and delivery," she said, and jerked her thumb toward the sled behind us. "I get the kids toys every year for Christmas."

I was perplexed. The puzzle pieces weren't fitting together for me—crazy woman appears out of nowhere and gives away toys to needy families. She fixed a stare on me, and then smiled.

"Thought I was poor and homeless, didn'tcha?" she smirked. I was appalled; was I really that transparent? "How many homeless people do you know with snowmobiles? Honestly, Arty, you crack me up."

She dismounted the Camel and started up the steps, then stopped, turned around, and barked, "Let's go, Arty! You're coming with me."

"Oh," I said, and hurried off the Sopwith Camel.

"Yo! Your Majesty! Bring the toys!" she commanded, shaking her head in disbelief, and I leapt back through the snow to the sled and retrieved the bag.

She knocked cheerily, and immediately a brunette holding a baby opened the door.

"Sky King!" she cried to my companion and gave her a warm embrace.

"Hey, Eunice," she replied, with obvious affection. "Is Harry ready?"

"Almost!" said the mother, and then she looked at me.

"Oh," said Sky King. "Allow me to introduce to you King Arthur."

"How nice," said Eunice, extending a firm handshake, and ushering us inside. "Always lovely to have more royalty around."

"Got some gifts for the kids," said Sky King, motioning to the bag.

"Oh, that's lovely! But you shouldn't have."

"Ah, but I should, and I want to. . . . After all, I can only give out of my abundance."

Give out of her abundance, I wondered. *What on Earth does that mean?*

"Well, it's dear of you and we're very grateful."

I looked around the house. These people didn't look poor at all. They certainly weren't rich, but the house was well furnished, clean, warm, and obviously well tended.

Eunice set the bag in a nearby closet. "Harry," she called. "Sky King's here!" She looked back at my companion. "He's so excited about going with you on the Sopwith Camel."

The whole county must be crazy, I thought.

Descending the stairs was a young boy I assumed to be Harry, arrayed in a long red velvet robe with fur-lined cuffs, and wearing a gold crown fashioned from cardboard and adorned with plastic beads. A tan corduroy and gold sequin-covered cigar box was tucked under his arm.

"Your lordship, King Harold," intoned Sky King, bowing and smoothly elbowing my rib to indicate that I was to do the same. Immediately I bowed, and Eunice curtsied.

King Harold giggled with delight and ran over to Sky King and delivered a big hug. And then he looked at me.

"Your Majesty," said Sky King very formally, "allow me to introduce to you Arthur, King of . . ." and she hesitated, not sure how to fill in the blank.

"Manhattan," I offered.

"Arthur, King of Manhattan." She smiled, pleased.

Good Lord, I thought; *I'm becoming one of them!*

"Pleased to meet you, King," said Harry, and he giggled again.

"Can't ride a Camel dressed like that," chided Sky King. "Let's you and me visit the mudroom and don some winter clothes for the ride." They trotted off around the corner.

Eunice and I were left alone. "I'm not really a King," I offered.

"The thought had occurred to me," she said brightly. "So, how long have you known Sky King?"

"About twenty minutes," I said. "My car broke down and she just happened by and picked me up."

"Oh . . ." she laughed. "Then you don't know . . ."

"Don't know what?"

"Who she really is."

"I just figured she was some poor crazy lady."

"Ah, you'd be wrong on both counts. Despite her eccentricities, sometimes I'm convinced she's the only sane person I know. And she most definitely is not poor."

I was puzzled.

"She's Mrs. Crawford. Mrs. Audrey Crawford. You know, of Crawford Textiles."

I did indeed know Crawford Textiles, and if this was true, Sky King was probably one of the wealthiest people in the country. "But . . ." I began.

"About twenty years ago when the mill went under, the town hit hard times. Sky King—that is, Mrs. Crawford—determined to ensure that no one here ever went without. So out of her considerable fortune she buys food and clothes and anything anyone needs. And no one ever has to so much as ask her; she just *knows*. I tell you, she's changed the town. In time the people regained hope and businesses came back. She saved us all. And although we aren't in dire *need* anymore, she continues to give to us all."

"But she's so . . ." I searched for the right word.

"Eccentric?" offered Eunice.

"Yes."

"I suppose so," she acknowledged. "She's always been unique. Her grandfather had been a pilot in the First World War and she loved planes. Her favorite TV show as a child was *Sky King* and she always insisted that people call her that. But most of her eccentricities can be attributed to the fact that she has rejected all of the things that the world says are important."

"Such as?"

"Such as money, power, and prestige. She often says that God has blessed her so greatly that she needs to give something back. She may be the only person I know who's not possessed by her possessions."

Possessed by possessions, I thought. *Was I possessed by my possessions?*

"All right, you two, I'm back; stop talking about me." Sky King reappeared along with Harry, now bundled up for his ride. "Well, then, let's go!" she said.

"You know, Sky King, we're going into town in a little bit with the big truck. We can take Arthur."

"Not a chance," was the reply. "He's coming with me. We kings have to stick together; right, Harry?" Little Harry nodded enthusiastically.

We tumbled out of the house and back into the cold night. Sky King mounted the Camel and Harry climbed on behind her with his cigar box. There was no room for me.

"Get on the sled," she ordered. I did, and she fired up the engine and off we went into the night.

As we rode along, my mind raced as I pondered all this craziness. I felt almost dizzy. Something inside was telling me that the real craziness was not this woman or the little boy. It was in me! I had gone mad with the pursuit of stuff that was never going to make me happy. I had amassed more money than I could ever imagine, but all it did was make me small, selfish, and hostile. But this woman had chosen something different. Perhaps she wasn't crazy at all; maybe the rest of us were.

We were in town now, and the setting was picturesque. Lights were strung from homes and trees, and the sparkly reflections on the snow made it look like a Christmas card come to life. A sign announced: *Village of Majestic. Population 545.* The snowmobile scooted down the main street and pulled up in front of a white clapboard church.

"Well, here we are," proclaimed Sky King, cutting the engine.

I stood in the snow and gazed at the church. My car was elsewhere, and there would be no fixing it tonight. All I could do was find a phone and call my wife—except that I didn't have the rental house number with me; I'd left it in the car.

"Yo, Arty," broke in Sky King. "It's time to get ready."

"Ready? For what?"

She didn't answer.

We walked through the front door of the church. Inside, it was a beehive of activity. People were scurrying back and forth. Most folks were dressed, well, *oddly*. A man with a turban wrapped around his head greeted me. Then a passing woman nearly knocked me over with her wings; she was followed by three little cherubs, literally, and it occurred to me that they were preparing to put on a Christmas pageant.

"Father Keeler! Merry Christmas!" Sky King greeted the young priest, who was making his way down the center aisle toward the vestibule where we stood.

"Sky King! A blessed Christmas to you."

"Father, I have some good news," said Sky King.

"I'd expect nothing else from you, my dear," he said playfully.

"I got us a third king."

"Oh?"

"Yes! Allow me to introduce to you Arthur, King of Manhattan." I smiled weakly and offered my hand.

"Welcome, Arthur, and thank you for filling in on such short notice. We are most grateful," said the priest.

Sky King whisked me away to a back room where people were putting the final touches on their costumes.

"I don't think this is such a good idea," I protested.

"You know, Arty, the only thing you ever give people is a hard time. Enough of that. Now get dressed," she ordered, handing me a pile of clothes consisting of a magenta robe, a long royal blue sleeveless vest adorned with gold braid and trim, and an immense gold crown. I dutifully donned them, and stood there feeling about as out of place and out of control as I ever have.

"Okay, here's the deal," said Sky King, now likewise arrayed. "I'm Myrrh." She pulled the empty bottle of perfume from her coat pocket. "Harry, here, is Frankincense . . ." On cue, Harry opened his cigar box and held up a small can of air freshener, wrapped in silvery mesh fabric, which he gleefully sprayed at me.

Lilacs, I thought.

"And you," she said, poking me in the ribs, "are Gold."

"And what do I bring?"

"You figure it out," she said.

We left the dressing room and made our way toward the back of the sanctuary. In the vestibule I stood waiting in place, staring at my feet, my mind reeling about what I was to bring, and what I was about to do in just a few moments, and marveling at the facts of the evening's odyssey, when a familiar voice broke into my thoughts.

"Arthur?"

I looked up. There stood Patrice with the girls.

"Daddy!" the girls cried, and circled me with hugs that nearly knocked me over.

Isn't it strange, the way even the most seemingly common moment can bring the most extraordinary insights. There I was, looking into the lovely, surprised face of my wife, my girls wrapped around me in an embrace, a typical sort of family moment for so many, and I felt grounded and sane for the first time in a very long time, garments and crown notwithstanding.

"What on earth?" said Patrice, alluding to my garb.

"It's a very long story," I said.

She gave me a tremendous hug and sighed. "I'm just glad you're all right. You mean more to me than anything."

I hugged her back and told her I loved her, and that right now I had to be Second King. The rest of the story would come later. She nodded in trusting resignation, and led the girls on into the sanctuary and slid with them into a pew. I was left with my two royal partners.

"Hey, there, Harry," I said. "Still have that box?" He nodded and handed me the cigar box.

I reached under my robe and took all the cash from my pocket and placed it in the box. It was my gold.

"Whoa, Arty, that's quite a roll," whispered Sky King.

The next thing I knew, we were off down the center aisle. Three kings. King Harry; Arthur, King of Manhattan; and Sky King. About as unlikely a trio as one would ever hope to see. We arrived at the manger and knelt down in front of the family. I was stunned to see that Jesus was a real baby. Gazing into the face of that child, something in me grew warm, and I felt full, whole, and healed.

We three earthly kings presented our gifts of air freshener, a wad of cash in a cigar box, and an empty perfume bottle. All of it utterly worthless to the Son of God. But for me, presenting these tokens became a moment of utter grace; the moment when I ceased to be possessed by my possessions and allowed myself to be possessed by something much richer, more powerful, and ultimately most satisfying. I let myself be possessed by the one true King, who is Jesus Christ. Possessed by his love, which may make the world look crazy, but ultimately gives us genuine hope and life. In stepping away from what had possessed me, and in giving up control, I was given the greatest gift of all by the greatest King of all.

12

I'LL BE HOME FOR CHRISTMAS

Jamie Radcliff sat in a chair looking at his father, Marshall, who was sitting across from him. Marshall Radcliff had been, in his prime, a corporate executive and a force to be reckoned with. His firm had built, or had a hand in building, practically every bridge, lock, and dam on the Ohio River. But you'd never know it now. He was thin, almost gaunt, and now in his mideighties, he was living in a fog.

Jamie and his sister, Beth, had moved their father to a nursing facility three years ago when it became obvious that their father couldn't live in the house anymore. Their mother had died a few years before that, and their father was becoming increasingly confused. Jamie got a call one day from a police officer who had pulled his father over for erratic driving and discovered that he didn't know where he was or how to get home. That's when they knew they had to move him.

The facility was nice enough, it was clean, and the food was decent, and the staff was always very friendly, but still it was a nursing facility. Marshall had his own room, and they had brought a few pieces of furniture from the house and had hung family photos on the wall. Not that it mattered, because Marshall couldn't recognize anyone in the photos, and for more than a year hadn't recognized his son or daughter, or any of his grandchildren when they came to visit. Most of the time, Marshall thought Jamie was *his* father.

Marshall stood up from his chair and looked out the window at the snow-covered central courtyard with its holly bushes and bird feeders.

"Well, look at that," he said. "We're passing Pike Island Dam. I built that in '61."

"Dad," said Jamie, "you're looking at the courtyard."

Marshall sat down and looked a little confused. "First job I was ever chief engineer," he said.

Marshall was riding the train. He liked being on the train, the gentle swaying motion of the Pullman car and the clickity-clack of wheels on the rails. He looked out the window at the familiar sights he knew all too well. The train was pulling into the station, and he recognized it as his hometown. They came to a slow stop, and Marshall got out. It was cold and snowy, but the air was very still and so he didn't mind. He walked into the station but found himself in the living room of his boyhood home. It was 1944, and he was fourteen.

It was Christmas Eve, but there wasn't much joy in the house. His mother was sitting in an armchair clutching a telegram she had received four weeks ago. It had barely left her hands since it was delivered. It was from the War Department and said that her husband, Marshall's father, was missing in action in Italy. They would contact her when and if they had more information.

The news had practically paralyzed his mother. Marshall and his older sister, Lydia, had pretty much taken over the house doing the cooking and cleaning, and they did manage to set up a Christmas tree and do some decorating, but their mother's grief threw a pall over the holiday.

Marshall's sister, Lydia, was determined to make everything as normal as possible.

"Mom, you need to eat something," she said, but got no response.

"Mom, don't give up hope. It just says Dad's missing; don't think the worst. It's Christmas. It's a time for miracles."

This did elicit a response from her mother, who clucked her tongue and said angrily, "Miracles? I've seen too much of life to believe in miracles."

Lydia made dinner and persuaded her mother to eat a little. At the dinner table Lydia said, "Christmas Eve service is at eight; you'd better get dressed, Mom."

Her mother looked at her incredulously. "Church? You think I'm going to church?"

Lydia, although only sixteen, was not to be trifled with. "Yes, Mom, we're going to church. I don't have a license, and it's too far to walk, and you're not going to ruin Marsh's and my Christmas. Go get dressed. We'll pray for Dad."

Her mother shook her head in silent desperation, but did as she was told.

Marshall wasn't feeling much like church either, but he knew not to rock the boat. So he put on his suit and the three of them went to church. Marshall's dad was mentioned in the prayers of the people, and during the announcements, Father Blake reminded the congregation to keep the missing soldier in prayer. To Marshall, it seemed so pointless. He had allowed his mother's despondency get to him.

The service ended, and a number of people came up to them with condolences. It was nice, but made it sound like he was already dead. Marshall remembers one elderly man who had been a veteran of the "Great War" tell them, "Never give up hope, and say your prayers."

They drove home through the snow-covered streets and parked the car in the driveway. They walked across the snowy lawn and up the porch steps. Lydia was the first one in the house and Marshall still remembers her screaming. Then she ran into the living room. Marshall was close behind and there was their father. All decked out in his captain's uniform and with his arm in a sling.

He kissed his kids and walked over to his wife and put his one good arm around her and held her for the longest time with tears streaming down their faces.

"I thought sometimes that I was never going to see you again," he said, "but I knew I couldn't give up hope."

"Never stop hoping," Marshall said.

"What's that, Dad?" said Jamie.

Marshall looked up at his son sitting across from him as if he didn't know how he got there.

That night at dinner, Jamie's wife, Carla, asked how the visit went.

"It's about the same," he said. "He doesn't know me, and he keeps thinking he's riding a train. Today he told me he could see the Pike Island Dam. It doesn't matter how many times I tell him he just doesn't know where he is. It's pretty depressing."

"Well," said Carla, "you never know what's going to happen. Don't give up hoping for the best."

"Funny," said Jamie, "That's what Dad said this afternoon."

Marshall was riding the train again.

He was wearing a white dinner jacket and black bow tie. The train pulled into a station he recognized as being in the town where he went to college. The train stopped, and he got off and entered the station and found himself at the college Christmas dance. It was 1952. McKinley College had gone coed in 1949, but there weren't many girls. When the college had dances, they invited the girls from a nearby girls' school. Consequently, most of those there weren't on dates, but rather danced with the girls who were there.

Marshall was standing next to his best friend, Bobby Langford, who had brought a flask and was doctoring their cups of punch. They surveyed their prospects for dance partners, most of whom were sitting on the other side of the room.

When he saw her, he got this odd tingle in his chest. She was petite and blonde and wearing a white tea-length dress with a crinoline petticoat that caused it to practically blossom from her waist. She was having an animated conversation with a friend. There was something about her that he found astonishingly attractive and that transcended her physical beauty.

"Who's that?" Marshall asked Bobby.

"Don't know, never seen her before but it's hard to believe that anybody that pretty isn't dancing."

"Do you think she's out of my league?" asked Marshall.

"Well," said Bobby, "if you don't ask her to dance, I will."

Marshall nervously made his way across the room. Because she was engaged in a conversation, she didn't see him until he was right next to her. She turned around and looked up at him. He remembers that she had the most beautiful blue eyes he had ever seen. His heart beat faster, and he realized that he was just standing there staring at her.

"Hello," she said and flashed him a huge smile.

He realized that he needed to say something. "Hello," he said, "I'm Marshall. Would I like to dance with me?" He knew he had said something wrong but couldn't figure it out. She began to laugh, but in a way that said she found his confusion flattering.

"Is English your second language?" She smiled at him.

"I feel like such an idiot," he said. "Would you like to dance?"

She bounced up and said, "I'd love to." She introduced herself as Delores, and they made small talk until the next song began. They stepped out onto the dance floor and the band began to play "You Belong to Me."

Whether it was a sign or not, the song was certainly fortuitous. They would be married two years later and in love the rest of their lives.

Later, much later, Delores would confess that she had seen Marshall and Bobby from across the room, but was hoping that Bobby would ask her to dance. Marshall always thought after that about how different his life would have been if he hadn't screwed up his courage and walked across that dance floor, instead letting Bobby have the first dance.

"Dad, Dad, Marshall?" Jamie had come for another visit and found his father sitting in his chair staring blankly into space.

"Oh, it's you," Marshall said, although it was obvious he didn't know who Jamie was. "I was just dancing with Delores."

"Dad you were not dancing with Delores."

"I most certainly was. She was wearing a white tea-length dress with a crinoline petticoat."

"Well, at least you're not riding the train," said Jamie.

Marshall looked at him incredulously, and said, "Well, how do you think I got there?"

Then he stood up, and looking out into the courtyard again, said, "Well, look at that, we're passing the Manchester Bridge. We blew that up one span at a time in 1970."

Jamie looked at him in disbelief. He knew the story. In fact he remembered his father taking the family to watch the first demolition. They had taken Jamie's grandmother, who was in a wheelchair, and that made them a little late. They parked the car, and the plan was to leave grandmother in the front seat. As they were getting out of the car, the explosives went off, and Jamie's dad used to joke that grandmother was the only one who saw it.

"Dad, if you blew it up in 1970, how can it be there now?"

Marshall became visibly agitated and looked at his son and said, "I think it's time for you to go."

Jamie felt like he'd been slapped, but he knew better than to argue at this point. He left the room and headed down the hall intending to leave the building, but, for some reason, when he got to the chapel, he ducked inside and sat down.

He wasn't much of a prayer, but as he sat there he thought, *This isn't fair. Such a vibrant, lovely, gifted man, and he's reduced to this.* A tear ran down his cheek. He felt so hopeless.

There was a second door to the chapel near the altar, and Jamie heard it open, and into the room came John Macpherson, a local clergy whom Jamie had actually gone to high school with.

John looked at him and said, "Oh, Jamie, I'm sorry. I didn't know there was anyone here." He noticed that Jamie was crying and said, "Hey, what's wrong?"

Whether it was the familiar face or something else, he didn't know, but the single tear turned into sobbing. John sat down next to him and put his hand on his shoulder.

When he got control, he said, "It's Dad." John didn't say anything. "It's just so hard to see him like this. He doesn't know who I am; he doesn't know his grandkids. It's all gone."

"What's gone?"

"All of the ball games we went to, the birthdays we celebrated, the Christmas trees we cut and decorated, all of it's gone."

John was quiet for a moment. "No, Jamie, it's not gone; it lives on in you and the kids and your sister and for all you know in him too. You never know what's going on inside him. What do you want?"

"I want him back."

"Now you're just being selfish."

This was not what Jamie wanted to hear. "Selfish, how dare you call me selfish when all I want is what's best for him."

"Jamie, you don't know what's best for him. I think you really want what's best for you, and that's to have your dad back. But he's not suffering, he's not agitated, he seems to be at peace."

"He thinks he's riding a train all the time," said Jamie.

John thought for a moment and then said, "Look, we're all riding a train. All of our destinies are uncertain. The idea that we get to choose where we're going is a fallacy. We'll never know how some small decision will forever change the course of our life. We think we're in control, but none of us ever is. Your father is just experiencing this writ large."

"He thinks he's riding a train," Jamie repeated.

"Look at me, Jamie." Jamie looked at his friend, who smiled and said, "Let him ride the train and better yet go with him. That's what Christmas is about. God sent his son to be one of us, to ride the train with us wherever it goes. To be a comfort, a companion, and to help us find our way when we get lost. Jamie, let him ride the train and go with him."

Marshall was on the train again. The cars were swaying gently and snow was falling. He looked out the windows at a very familiar town. The train slowly stopped, and Marshall got out. He crossed the platform and went into the station, where he found himself in the sanctuary of the church in the town they had lived in in the late '50s. It was decorated for Christmas. Huge wreaths hung from the walls; candles were lit in the windows. The advent wreath had all the candles, including the Christmas candle, lit. Marshall knew what was happening right away.

This was the annual Christmas pageant. It was 1959. The church had a tradition of doing the pageant on Christmas Eve, and another tradition was that the youngest child in the church played the infant Jesus. Jamie had been born in November and was to be the infant star.

Marshall walked down the aisle and took his seat next to Delores, who took his hand, looked at him like, "Isn't this so exciting?"

The Church of the Nativity was a large church built in the Norman style, with impossibly high ceilings and a transept that was large enough for a veritable Christmas pageant extravaganza. The production was so over the top that the congregation swelled to twice its size as the community came to watch the spectacle. Children were certainly involved in the minor parts of shepherds and angels and townspeople, but adults did all the speaking roles. And since bigger was better, this production included live animals. The shepherds had several real sheep, and Mary and Joseph entered the sanctuary with Mary riding a real donkey down the center aisle. The rector drew the line at the Magi having a real camel.

The narrator was reading from Luke: ". . . and while they were there the time came for her to give birth. And she gave birth to her firstborn son and wrapped him in swaddling cloths."

And Jamie was brought out by an angel. Marshall looked at his recently born son and said to himself, "I'm going to do right by him. I'm going to love him and comfort him," and then he prayed. "Heavenly Father, make me a good dad."

When it came time for the shepherds to receive their announcement from the angels, one of the sheep got spooked and dragged little Timmy Regal down the center aisle until his father rescued him. But other than that, it was a perfect evening.

It was Christmas Eve, and Jamie and Carla were having an early dinner with their kids before going to church. Jamie began to think about how many important events were tied to Christmas.

"You know," he said, "in 1944 my grandmother received a telegram that my grandfather was missing in action in Italy," and he told them the story about how his grandfather showed up unexpectedly on Christmas Eve.

Then he told them the story about how his mother and father met at a Christmas dance and that his mother was actually more interested in his father's friend than in his father.

And then he told the story about how, as a six-week-old infant, he played the baby Jesus, and how a sheep dragged a little boy down the aisle of the church.

He thought to himself, *John was right. It's all here. It's here right with me.*"

After dinner, Jamie was loading the dishwasher while Carla got the kids ready. She had to be at the church early because the kids were in the pageant.

When they came downstairs, Jamie said, "You go along. I'm going to stop and see Dad. I'll meet you there."

Jamie drove through the snow-covered streets of this sleepy little town he had grown up in and all sorts of other memories of Christmas came cascading through his mind. He parked the car, entered the home, and walked down the hallway to his father's room.

His father was lying in bed in his pajamas.

"Hi, Dad. Merry Christmas."

"Merry Christmas, Jamie," his father replied.

Jamie was stunned. He hadn't called him by name or recognized him in more than a year. "How you feeling, Dad?"

"I feel great."

Then Jamie took a bit of a risk. "Taken the train anywhere lately?"

"As a matter of fact, I have. I went to the Christmas pageant in 1959 when you played Jesus. It was wonderful."

Jamie smiled. "I wish I could have gone with you."

"But you were with me," his father said. "Do you really think I can go anywhere without you? After your mom, you and your sister are the most important people in my life. You're always with me."

Jamie wasn't sure what to say, but then his father filled the silence.

"I'm going away soon."

"Oh?" said Jamie. "Where?"

"Well, that's the odd thing. I usually know where I'm going, but not this time. So I'm expecting a real adventure."

"Well, good," said Jamie, "you have a good time." He was acting on John's advice now.

"I'm sure I will," said Marshall, "but something tells me I may not be coming back."

"Well, I suppose if you find a place you really like it would probably be okay to stay a while," said Jamie.

"Exactly what I thought, too," said Marshall.

"I love you, Dad."

"I love you too, Jamie, and you tell Carla and the kids and your sister, Beth, and her brood that I love them all very much."

"I will. I have to go now. The kids are in the pageant at church."

"I have to go now, too," said Marshall, and he closed his eyes.

Jamie kissed his father on the forehead.

Jamie drove to the church, thanking God for this minor miracle he had just experienced. He didn't know where his father was going; all he knew was that for the first time in months he was at peace.

He arrived at the church and slid into the pew with Carla and told her what happened, and the pageant began. The risk factor was lowered exponentially because of the absence of live animals.

Jamie's two daughters were angels and as he watched them singing, he prayed, "Lord, make me a good dad."

Marshall was riding the train. There was snow outside falling gently as the train made its way down the tracks. He was wearing a white dinner jacket and a black bow tie, and he felt more alive than he had ever felt in his life. In fact, he felt positively transformed. He had no idea where he was going, but the scenery he passed in the waning sunlight looked simultaneously familiar and unfamiliar. As if it had been described to him once or he had read about it.

The train pulled in the station, which was decorated for Christmas. He knew that this was his stop. He looked out at the platform and there were all sorts of people he recognized. There was his father in his captain's uniform walking arm in arm with his mother. There were men he had worked with fifty years before and people he had attended high school and college with. But he didn't see *her*.

He made his way down the aisle of the car and down the stairs to the platform. He wasn't sure where to go or what to do next.

"Marshall," he heard his name called.

He turned around and there she was, a petite blonde with fierce blue eyes. She was wearing a white tea-length dress with a crinoline petticoat that caused it to blossom from her waist. She ran to him, threw her arms around him, kissed him gently, and said, "Welcome home."

We're all riding the train. But we don't ride it alone. We travel with family and friends and sometimes even with people we don't like all that much. We think we know where we're going, but we really don't. We never know how some angry word or kind gesture or even some random act, like asking a girl to dance, might change our lives (and the lives of others) forever.

Christmas is about the incarnation. God became flesh and dwelt among us. And there's a sense in which Jesus is riding with us too. To be our companion, and comforter, to show us the way when we get lost, and ultimately, to bring us home.

END

ABOUT THE AUTHOR

Jim Simons is a Pittsburgh native and has been a priest of the Episcopal Church since 1985. He has served the past twenty-six years as the Rector of St. Michael's of the Valley in Ligonier, Pennsylvania.